GRAYSLAKE AREA PUBLIC LIBRARY

3 6109 00488

W9-AAT-037

# A WICKED KISS

(Wicked Book 2)

By M.S. Parker

GRAYSLAKE AREA PUBLIC LIBRARY
100 Library Lane
Grayslake, IL 60030

This book is a work of fiction. The names, characters, places and incidents are products of the writer's imagination or have been used fictitiously and are not to be construed as real. Any resemblance to persons, living or dead, actual events, locales or organizations is entirely coincidental.

Copyright © 2015 Belmonte Publishing

Published by Belmonte Publishing.

All rights reserved. Without limiting the rights under copyright reserved above, no part of this publication may be reproduced, stored in or introduced into a retrieval system, or transmitted, in any form, or by any means (electronic, mechanical, photocopying, recording, or otherwise) without the prior written permission of the copyright owner.

The author acknowledges the trademarked status and trademark owners of various products referenced in this work of fiction, which have been used without permission. The publication/use of these trademarks is not authorized, associated with, or sponsored by the trademark owners.

ISBN-13: 978-1517041496

ISBN-10: 151704149X

Rom
Parker,
M.S.
9-15

3 6109 00488 6708

# Chapter 1

I didn't know what to do. Three months ago, my husband, Allen Lockwood, had died in what I'd thought – what everyone had thought – was a freak accident. I'd been with Allen for eight years and losing him had nearly killed me. I'd had to fight my way back through grief, through legal battles with my late husband's asshole relatives, through deciding what I wanted to do with the rest of my life now that everything had gone ass-end-up.

I was a widow at twenty-six. I'd met Allen my freshman year of college and while I'd continued pursuing my degree in early childhood education, all of my plans for the future had included him from nearly that moment on. Marriage, children...

I winced and closed my eyes. Just before Allen died, we'd talked about starting a family. For a few weeks after the...accident, I'd even worried that I was pregnant.

Hoped.

Worried.

Hoped.

I sighed. I hadn't been pregnant and I still didn't know if I was happy or sad that I wasn't carrying Allen's child. What I did know was that it had added a layer of stress that I hadn't needed at the time.

And then had come the insurance policy, the million dollar one that I never knew anything about. That had been the first hint that Allen had been hiding things from me.

Jasper had told me that it was nothing, that Allen had probably taken out the policy because he'd known that his parents and siblings would fight me for the vineyard where we'd been living together since I'd graduated from college and he'd wanted me to have something until the legal shit was worked out.

Yeah, Jasper.

Fucking bastard.

Jasper Whitehall had been Allen's college roommate and his best friend. He'd been my rock through this whole ordeal. The first person I'd called after the skydiving 'accident' that had taken Allen's life. The person who'd taken care of me when I'd wandered around outside without sunscreen and ended up giving myself heat stroke and had nearly burned my skin off. He'd been the one who'd come when Gregory and May Lockwood had hired someone to set part of my vineyard on fire. He'd stayed with me when I hadn't wanted to stay alone.

And I'd slept with him last night.

It had been a stupid, stupid mistake. We'd gone out for celebratory drinks after a judge had a

2

surprisingly ruled in my favor against my former in-laws regarding the vineyard. The court was still waiting to rule on Allen's trust. I didn't care about that though. His parents thought I did, but I'd never cared about the money. Despite Allen's multi-million dollar trust-fund, I'd always worked. Teaching second grade didn't pay much, but I loved it, and if I needed it to be enough, it would be.

Now, even without the trust-fund, I had more than enough thanks to the million dollar insurance policy. A policy I didn't want and had already decided to donate to charity.

To Jasper. To fund the low-income health clinic he'd always wanted to start.

I'd decided to give it to him because he was a good doctor, because Allen had wanted to give him money from the frozen trust, and because I knew it would piss Gregory and May off.

But I mostly wanted to do it because he was a good man.

Or so I'd thought.

I'd been a bit drunk last night...well, okay, more than a bit, and he'd tried to stop me from coming on to him. And that was the truth. I'd kissed him first. I'd begged him to sleep with me. I'd wanted sex. I'd wanted him.

He'd been amazing, and not just in the sense of the quality and quantity of orgasms he'd provided. He'd told me to let go, had asked me to let him take care of me. And I'd been dumb enough to trust him.

Tears burned in my eyes and I swiped at them. I'd trusted him and I'd trusted Allen.

And they'd both betrayed me.

I tossed the letter onto the nearby table. I didn't want to read it again. I didn't need to read it again. The words were indelibly imprinted on my brain. Allen had written me a letter before he died. A letter that had gotten lost in the mail.

A letter where he told me that he'd lied to me, that he'd betrayed everything we'd been about as his last act on earth. A letter where he'd confessed to having been diagnosed with a fatal disease. No cure and fast-acting. A disease he hadn't wanted to tell me about because he hadn't wanted me to deal with it.

So he'd killed himself.

He'd needed to make it look like an accident for the insurance to pay out, and he'd definitely done that. Until a few minutes ago, I'd thought that his parachute hadn't opened and that had been why he died. While that was still technically true, I knew now that he'd done it on purpose. He'd killed himself quickly and with witnesses to ensure that no one would think it had been intentional.

And Jasper had helped him do it.

The tears spilled over then and the pain in my heart that had begun to fade as time passed came back. And it brought friends.

That's what I'd thought Jasper was. A friend. At the very least, I'd thought he was that.

But he'd known.

He hadn't helped Allen die in the sense of providing him the means to die, or setting it up so that his parachute didn't open. He hadn't killed

4

Allen, but he'd known about the disease. He'd given Allen a clean bill of health so my husband could buy the secret insurance policy.

Hell, for all I knew, he'd told Allen the best way to kill himself to ensure that there was no way the medical examiner would be able to diagnose the disease. Free falling thousands of feet had done it.

I was going to throw up.

The fact that I'd slept with the lying bastard was enough to make me run the last few steps and land on my knees next to the toilet where I heaved vomit, bile and what was left of my heart into the sewer.

I forced myself to shower again. I needed the time to collect myself as much as I needed to feel clean after getting sick. I'd argued with myself for the entire duration of the shower, trying to decide what I should do. It was a Saturday, which meant I didn't need to go to work so I didn't have that excuse. I actually had to make a decision.

I wanted to scream at Allen, yell at him for what he'd done. For lying to me. For making me watch him die in that horrible way.

But Allen wasn't here. Allen was dead.

Allen had chosen to be dead.

He'd chosen to leave me even after all of the promises we'd made to each other. We'd promised sickness as well as health, worse as well as better. We'd promised to be together until death parted us, but we'd always assumed – or at least I had always assumed – that we'd have no choice in the matter. What Allen had done had been the same, in my mind, as leaving me.

He'd left me.

Anger followed the pain, and I let it come.

Being angry at what he'd done was easier than being hurt over it.

I just wanted to aim the negative feelings at someone, and since Allen wasn't here, I had to go with the other option. By the time I was dressed, I'd successfully managed to transfer all of that anger onto Jasper.

I'd seen the building where Jasper worked with his father, but I'd never been inside. Today, I walked in and went straight to the receptionist.

She looked to be in her early thirties, but wasn't taking it well. She dressed like she was trying to look ten years younger, complete with make-up. Even her sienna-colored hair was cut into a short style that was designed for someone a bit younger.

"Hi." I forced myself to be polite. "I need to talk to Jasper."

Her light brown eyes narrowed and her lips pursed. "Dr. Whitehall is busy right now."

"Then I'll wait."

She looked back down at whatever it was she was working on and I knew she fully expected me to join the others in the chairs until I got tired of waiting and left. Instead, I crossed my arms and glared at her. I usually tried to be polite to people, especially ones who had to interact with the public, but I had a feeling this was the same woman who'd given me a hard time about talking to Jasper the day of the fire.

"You can have a seat over there." Her tone was

sharp.

"I'm fine here. Thanks."

After another minute or so, she apparently figured out I wasn't going to budge because she pushed herself up from the desk and walked off in a huff. I told myself I'd wait ten minutes and if she didn't return with Jasper, I was going in the back to find him.

"Georgia, if someone is giving you a problem, you should call..." Jasper's voice trailed off as he stepped out into the waiting room and saw me.

For a moment, I forgot about the letter, about the anger, about how he'd deceived me. All I saw was the thick, coal black hair that I knew would be soft to the touch. The clear gray eyes that I'd seen dark with desire just last night. The six foot tall, muscular frame that I'd felt wrapped around me, protecting me.

"Shae."

The way he said my name, so full of...something I didn't want...everything came rushing back.

"We need to talk," I snapped.

His eyes widened slightly in surprise, and caution replaced the happiness I'd seen. "This way." He opened the door and motioned for me to follow him.

"Dr. Whitehall," Georgia called from the other side of her desk. "You have patients waiting."

He didn't even look at her, but I did, and what I saw on her face confirmed what I'd suspected. She wanted him. While that explained how she treated me, it certainly didn't excuse it. But that wasn't my problem at the moment.

My problem was ushering me into a small side room and closing the door behind us.

"I'm sorry I had to leave this morning," he said as soon as the door closed. "I couldn't call off today and I didn't want to wake you up to have this conversation—"

"We're not talking about that," I cut him off.

Confusion passed across his face and he took a step back. "Shae, what's wrong? Did the Lockwoods—?"

"I'm not here about the fucking Lockwoods!" My temper finally snapped. I curled my hands into fists to stop them from shaking. "I'm here about what you did."

"What I did?" He reached out a hand towards me and it hovered there for a moment before dropping back to his side. "Shae, I don't understand."

"Allen mailed me a letter." My voice wavered. "The post office lost it so I didn't get it until today."

"Oh, Shae."

Understanding filled his eyes and I knew he thought I was upset because of the reminder, especially after what had happened between us.

"You bastard," I whispered as my eyes filled with tears. I'd told myself that I wasn't going to cry, but I couldn't seem to stop myself.

"I'm so sorry." He raked his hand through his hair. "I never should have...I knew it was wrong, I just...shit."

I ignored what he was saying. I knew he still

didn't get it. "You lying son of a bitch."

"Lying?" His eyes shot up in surprise.

"Allen confessed in the letter." The knot in my stomach twisted. "He said he was sick and that he didn't want to live like that."

The color drained from his face, confirming what I'd read.

"You knew." The words stuck in my throat and I had to spit them out. "You knew he was dying! You knew he was going to kill himself!"

"Shae, I—" He took a step towards me.

I held up my hand and backed away. "No. No more." I shook my head. "I can't take anymore of this. I don't ever want to see you or talk to you again. Stay away from me."

I didn't wait for him to say anything. There wasn't anything he could say. No explanation I wanted to hear. Nothing that would make this better. Nothing could make this better.

# Chapter 2

I went home, but I didn't do anything. Oh, I tried, I just couldn't seem to focus. I wandered from room to room, starting to do something and then forgetting what it was right in the middle of it. Time seemed to move in fits and starts. I kept seeing the accident...the suicide, all over again. Seeing Allen die. And then I'd see Jasper. Comforting me. Being there for me.

Kissing me.

Lying to me.

Had he been sitting by the phone that day, waiting for my call? Had Allen called him that morning before we'd left so he could say goodbye? Had Jasper already been grieving when I'd called?

And what if the motivation had been less pure than Jasper's friendship? Was it possible that he'd agreed to mess with Allen's medical records with the intent of convincing me to hand over the insurance policy? Was that what the million dollars from Allen's trust had been for in the first place? A payment to Jasper for covering things up?

I found myself standing in front of the fireplace in the living room, staring at the pictures on the mantle. There was one from a college party, the first picture Allen and I had taken together. We'd been dating for two weeks at that point. Our first Christmas together. College graduation, both his and mine. Our engagement picture. The day I'd moved in with him. Our first Christmas in the vineyard. Our wedding.

I stomped into the kitchen, my hands shaking with the enormity of what I was feeling. I couldn't look at him, couldn't see his face everywhere. I didn't want him to be here anymore.

I grabbed a trash bag and went back into the living room. I didn't take my time to remove the pictures from the frames, to carefully set aside the photos. I didn't do any of the things I'd always thought I'd do when I'd finally gotten the strength to start putting pictures away.

With one sweep across the mantle, I knocked the pictures into my trash bag.

The ones on the wall followed. I heard the glass breaking as I dropped frame after frame into the bag. The ones that were too big to fit came down and sat next to the door so I could take them out to the trash.

When I finished with the pictures, I carried everything out to trash cans. The ones that I didn't have room for went on the ground next to the cans. It took three trips to get everything out and by the time I finished, I was sweaty and hot, but I told myself it was worth it.

But when I was in the shower for the third time that day, the adrenaline that had fueled my semi-cleaning spree faded away and I could no longer deny the emptiness inside me. I crumpled to the floor, pulling my knees tight against my chest as I gave in to the tears.

It was like losing Allen all over again, except this time, I didn't have the comfort of memories. All of my memories were now tainted with his deceit. After Allen died, it had been horrible, but I'd had those eight precious years to hold on to. They hadn't been perfect. We'd fought, of course. Sometimes it had been his fault, sometimes mine, but we'd always worked things out.

That's what made this so much worse, I realized. There was no chance of resolution. No way to confront him and demand an answer. No way for him to know how badly he'd hurt me. There would be no explanation, no apologies or forgiveness. There'd be no making up, or the relief that came with it.

I would be forced to carry this knowledge without the benefit of knowing why, without any chance at resolution.

I pressed my face tighter against my knees. "Why, Allen?" I whispered even though I knew there'd be no answer.

I stayed in the shower until the water ran cold. I was shivering as I dried off and decided on my favorite robe instead of clothes. It was big and soft, the same cobalt blue as my eyes, and best of all, it was warm.

My stomach growled and I realized that it was almost six o'clock, but I hadn't eaten anything all day. I headed downstairs to the kitchen and made myself a grilled cheese sandwich. That, plus a cold beer, went a long way to making me almost feel better.

I was just finishing up both when I heard a noise from the front of the house. I grabbed the house phone from the counter and headed towards the living room. With its big picture window, I'd be able to see enough to know if I should call the police. My fingers were on the buttons when I saw the tall, shadowy figure, but a moment later, I recognized him and I dropped the phone onto the couch.

I flung the door open and was halfway down the steps before I remembered that I wasn't wearing shoes. I didn't care.

"What the hell are you doing here?"

Jasper froze. He'd been walking back to his car, I saw now. If I'd waited just a few more minutes, he would've left. For a moment, I almost wished I had. He slowly turned and I saw he had a bouquet of flowers in his hands.

"What are those?" My mouth was suddenly dry.

"Whenever Allen screwed up, he said he'd buy you lilies because that was the first flower he'd ever bought for you."

I folded my arms across my chest as a pain went through me. Jasper came towards me, holding out the flowers. They weren't lilies, I saw with some relief. Then my eyes narrowed as he came close enough for me to identify what they were.

14

"Lisianthus," he said. "I remembered that these were your favorite."

I automatically reached out to accept them. It was a beautiful arrangement, rich purple flowers mixed with white baby's breath.

"You remembered?" I whispered as I lightly touched the petals. Lisianthus resembled tulips and weren't the usual kind of flowers women expected.

"You mentioned once that they had been your mom's favorite too."

I'd mentioned. *Mentioned.* And he remembered. Tears pricked at my eyelids. Allen had known that too and had gotten them for me on occasion, but the lilies had been a thing between us, special in their own way. Jasper hadn't tried to take that from me, but had brought me what he remembered I liked.

"Will you please let me explain?" There was a note of near-desperation in his voice.

I looked up, but twilight had fallen and Jasper's face was shadowed.

"Please, Shae. You can kick me out after and I'll never bother you again. Just let me explain."

My heart twisted at the thought of never seeing Jasper again. Of never knowing. I was still angry with him, but I knew I needed to hear what he had to say. He was the only one who could provide me with any kind of answers, even if they weren't the ones I wanted.

"Come in." I shivered as a gust of wind blew across us.

I went back inside, going straight for the kitchen without a glance behind to see if he was following. I got a vase from one of the bottom cabinets and filled it with water. When I turned back around, Jasper was standing there, his hands shoved into his pockets, a haggard expression on his face.

"Let's go sit," I said, carrying the vase with me back into the living room. He followed without a word, waiting until I'd sat down in one of the chairs before taking a seat on the couch.

"What I did..." he began and then shook his head. "I knew he was sick. I'm the one who sent him to the specialists. And yes, I kept it from you." He looked up at me. "Because Allen asked me to."

"I knew that already." My nails were digging into my palms, every muscle in my body tense.

"He didn't want you to pity him."

I blinked. "What?"

Jasper leaned forward in his chair. "Allen loved you more than anything and he didn't want you to pity him. That's why he asked me to keep it from you. It's a horrible disease, Shae." His voice caught and he cleared his throat. "I didn't want to see my friend like that, and I knew he didn't want you to see him that way."

"He was my husband, Jasper. That wasn't your decision to make." The words came out more sharply than I'd intended.

"You're right," he agreed. "But he asked me to. And I'm a doctor, Shae. I couldn't do it, personally or professionally."

"Fuck profession," I snapped. I could feel the tears again and tried to force them back. "I thought you were my friend. You said you were. But you sat

16

here and lied to me every day. You let me think it was an accident."

"I didn't know," he said quietly. "He asked me to keep his illness from you, and he asked me to give him old medical records from before the diagnosis. I suspected he wanted it because of insurance, but I didn't ask."

"So you weren't surprised when I got that call?"

He hesitated and then shook his head. "Not really." He looked down at his hands. "And that's when I started to suspect what he'd done."

"You knew."

"Not for sure, no. He didn't tell me what he was planning, I swear. It wasn't until afterwards that I thought it was possible."

"But you still didn't tell me."

He looked up and I almost winced at the pain in his eyes. "Of course not. I couldn't do that to you."

"So you just let me think that it was an accident."

He stood suddenly and came over to where I was sitting. He dropped to his knees in front of me. His hands covered mine. Part of me wanted to pull away, but a bigger part didn't.

"What good would it have done to tell you what I suspected?" he asked. His hands tightened around mine. "You were hurting so badly, and Allen's family was being..." He shook his head. "I couldn't do that to you."

"Couldn't tell me the truth?" I didn't want him to have a noble reason, didn't want to forgive him. I wanted to be angry because it was easier than being

17

hurt, because he was here and Allen wasn't.

"I couldn't be the one to tell you what Allen had done." He turned his head away, but I could still see emotions play across his face. "I was afraid."

Something had shifted in our conversation and I didn't know where it was going next.

"Afraid of what?" I asked.

He was so quiet that I thought he wasn't going to answer, but when he finally did, his words were so soft that I almost missed them.

"I was afraid that you'd hate me and I'd lose you. I'd just lost Allen. I couldn't...I'm sorry. It was selfish and wrong."

Images flashed through my mind. Jasper giving me strength at Allen's funeral. Standing with me against the Lockwoods. Holding my hand in court. The blurry day I'd gotten heat stroke. How he'd dropped everything the day of the fire. Tending to my feet. The way he'd looked at me when I'd called him only Allen's friend. Just before I'd kissed him.

He started to stand, but I grabbed his hands, pulling him back down onto his knees. He looked at me, startled.

I needed to hear him say it.

"Why didn't you tell me, Jasper?" I asked. My fingers tightened around his hands. "The whole truth this time."

"I couldn't hurt you like that, Shae." He gave me a sad smile. "I care about you too much."

It was suddenly hard to breathe. I'd known it. Of course I had.

He laughed, the sound bitter. "And I fucked it up

anyway, didn't I? I wanted to protect you. Take care of you. And I'm the one who hurt you." He pulled his hands away from mine and stood. "I won't do it again."

He took a step and then stopped when I spoke.

"Then don't."

He didn't look at me, but he didn't keep going either.

"Don't leave me."

# Chapter 3

"Shae?"

My name was so much more than a question.

"I don't want to lose you either."

He turned then and his eyes were blazing. "You'll never lose me, Shae." He went to his knees in front of me again and reached out to cup my face between his hands. "Please forgive me."

I put one hand over his. It wasn't even a question. "Forgiven."

His entire body slumped in relief. He leaned forward until his forehead rested against mine. "I was so scared that you would never forgive me." He pushed my wet hair back from my face. "I thought for sure you'd think last night..." His voice trailed off and he suddenly pulled back. "I shouldn't have...I mean...."

"Jas." I reached out and put my hand on his cheek. When my thumb brushed against his bottom lip, he sucked in a breath. "Stop talking."

He swallowed hard and I could feel the tension

in his body.

"You said that you wanted to take care of me." My heart was racing, but I knew that only part of it was from nerves.

"Yes."

I leaned forward until my lips barely brushed against his. "Then take care of me."

"Shae," he groaned my name, but didn't move.

"Unless you don't want..." I started to pull back, wondering if it was possible I'd misread him.

He surged forward, cutting off the rest of what I'd planned on saying. Whatever those words had been flew out of my head as his mouth covered mine. He buried his fingers in my hair, his teeth scraping at my bottom lip. He parted my lips, his tongue curling around mine. There was none of the hesitation from last night. He claimed my mouth with a need that made my entire body glow.

My head fell back as he kissed his way down my neck. Then his hands were pushing aside my robe, fingers leaving trails of heat across my skin. My nipples hardened as the cool air caressed me and I shivered. Then his mouth was on me, hot and wet as his tongue teased my nipple. My back arched as pleasure went straight through me.

Everything I'd been feeling, worrying about, all of it disappeared. I knew it'd be back, but for right now, it was gone. All I felt was the heat of Jasper's mouth and hands, the feel of his skin sliding over mine. All I knew was that I loved the way he made me feel.

He released my nipple and kissed his way down

my stomach until he was pulling my legs over his shoulders and leaning down to press his mouth against me. I let out a sound halfway between a wail and a moan as his tongue moved over my pussy. His fingers tightened on my hips, holding me still as he kissed me with the same possessive enthusiasm he'd used on my mouth earlier.

"Jas," I called out his name as I came for the first time. He slid his fingers inside me even as my body was still spasming. I made a half-strangled sound as he began to thrust them in a slow and steady rhythm.

"Come on, baby," he murmured. He flicked out his tongue against my clit. "Come for me again."

"Jas," I breathed his name this time. His name. A surreal feeling washed over me and I expected guilt to follow. Guilt that his name came so easily to my lips.

But I didn't feel guilty. I just felt glad that he was here. Happy that this man hadn't left me. That he cared about me.

"Just breathe." He pressed his lips against the inside of my thigh. "Let go, Shae. I've got you."

He curled his fingers, easily finding that spot inside me. My back arched as he pressed against it and white spots danced behind my eyes.

"I've got you, baby."

He sucked my clit into his mouth even as he rubbed the tips of his fingers against me. I buried my hand in his hair as my body tightened with another orgasm. I cried out as I came, writhing against his hand and mouth as he kept working me through a climax that left every inch of me throbbing.

My head was still spinning when he picked me up. My arms went around his neck and I rested my head on his chest. I closed my eyes and breathed in the scent of him, the smell of antiseptic from work, of his laundry detergent and fabric softener. The scent that was simply Jasper.

A lump formed in my throat as I realized I couldn't remember what Allen had smelled like. I knew the detergent, the fabric softener. I knew the smell of the vineyard. But I couldn't remember the part that was just him.

I turned my face away as Jasper placed me on my bed. I didn't want him to see the tears and think he'd caused them. The lighting was dim enough that I thought it would work, but I hadn't realized how much he truly saw.

"Shae." Jasper's voice was soft as he cupped my chin and turned my face back towards him.

I hadn't realized I'd started crying until I felt him wiping away my tears. And then he was gathering me into his arms, pulling me back against his chest. He tucked my robe more tightly around me and pressed his lips against my temple.

"I'm sorry, Shae."

"You didn't do anything wrong." I sniffled.

"Then what is it?"

I shook my head. I couldn't talk about it. Not with him.

"It's okay, Shae." His hand slid beneath my robe to rest on my stomach. There was nothing sexual

24

about his touch now, only comfort. "You can talk to me about anything." His fingers made soothing circles on my stomach. "Even Allen. It's okay."

"I don't want to talk right now." I twisted my head around so I could see him. "Please, Jasper."

"Whatever you want." He tucked some hair behind my ear. "I'm here."

I turned in his arms and put my hand on his face. The stubble on his cheek was rough against my palm. I didn't know what this thing was between us, or even if I wanted to define it, but there was one thing I needed to be clear about.

"I want you." I slid my hand down his chest and cupped him. He was so hard that it had to be painful, and yet I knew he'd walk away if I asked him to.

"Are you sure?" The words were strained.

I didn't bother with an answer. Not a verbal one anyway. I unzipped his pants and slipped my hand inside. His long eyelashes fluttered as I wrapped my fingers around him. Heat spread through me and I began to stroke him. He swelled even more under my touch and my stomach twisted. I hadn't realized just how much I wanted him until now.

I hooked my leg over his waist, shifting until the tip of his cock brushed against me.

"Shae," he groaned my name as he put his hands on my shoulders. "We need..."

I shook my head. "No. It's okay." I slid the head inside me and we both moaned. "Please."

His lips found mine. "Anything," he breathed the word before he kissed me.

25

He pushed his hips up, burying himself inside me. I was still wet from what he'd done before and he slid into me easily. I clutched him to me as our bodies moved together. The kiss became hard and fierce, his teeth nipping at my bottom lip. The base of his cock rubbed against my clit, sending near-painful shivers of sensation through me. I whimpered, biting down on his lip.

Jasper made a sound low in his throat and then he was flipping us, driving hard and deep into me until I exploded. My nails dug into the back of his shirt, clawing at the material. He pressed his face against the side of my neck, teeth worrying at the skin until I knew he was leaving a mark. I didn't care though. I just wanted him.

And then he was coming too, his cock pulsing and emptying inside me.

At some point, we disentangled and cleaned up, but Jasper didn't say that he needed to go, and I didn't ask him to stay. Instead, we slid under the covers and he wrapped his arms around me, neither of us having to say a word to know that we both needed to be held.

Finally, I broke the silence. "I can't accept the money, Jas."

"It's okay." He pulled me tighter to him.

We were both naked and the feel of his skin against mine warmed me in a way that had nothing to do with temperature. And it wasn't sex either, at least not right now. He warmed something inside me that had been frozen since Allen died.

"I don't want to do that to you," I said.

"It doesn't matter, Shae. I'll get the money for the clinic some other way. I've been saving for it. I'll just keep on that plan." He kissed the spot under my ear that made me shiver. "You do whatever you need to do."

We fell silent again. My fingers traced patterns on his arm and I just let myself relax. Relax into his embrace, into his body. I could feel his heartbeat against my back, feel him breathing.

"I wish I hadn't thrown away my pictures," I spoke softly, not really expecting an answer.

"You didn't," he murmured. His voice was thick with sleep. "I put them in my car. But most of your frames were fucked." He kissed my temple. "It's all okay."

"You saved my pictures?" I looked over my shoulder, but Jasper's face was turned away. I waited for a moment, listening. He was asleep.

He'd saved my pictures. I put my hands on his, tracing each long, strong finger. I'd had these fingers inside me, pleasuring me, and I'd had them gentle and healing on me. He was so many things I'd never expected. How had I not seen this side of him before?

I pushed away all of the confusing thoughts that were threatening to crowd in and ruin this. I wasn't going to read too much into things, wasn't going to start wondering what this meant. I didn't need to analyze whatever this was. If Jasper wasn't asking me to define what we were, I didn't need to press the issue myself. I needed to just let things be right now. No pressure. I needed one thing in my life that wasn't complex, wasn't complicated. I needed something easy and reassuring.

Jasper was that. He didn't try to make me think about things. He just made me feel. Feel something other than anger and hurt. He made me feel alive and made me forget everything else. He was here for me, and I never wanted to lose that. I never wanted to lose him.

I swallowed hard at the realization. I'd never expected him to mean so much to me, but there it was. It was probably crazy and way too soon. It was probably a horrible idea.

But it was too late. We could slow things down, but what had happened between us over the last two days changed everything.

I just hoped it would be for the better.

# Chapter 4

It was a strange thing, going from friends to lovers, or at least it should've been. With Jasper though, it felt natural. He woke up next to me on Sunday morning and it wasn't weird. Maybe it was because he didn't let it get that way. He didn't rush out or try to snuggle closer. Instead, he climbed out of bed, pulled on the clothes he'd discarded at some point during the night and went into the bathroom.

After that, he made me breakfast. Like a for-real breakfast of pancakes and bacon and scrambled eggs. After breakfast, he helped me bring in the pictures from his car and salvage what frames I could. We talked, but not about what us having slept together – again – meant, but I didn't feel like we needed to talk about it. Whatever this was between us was good, and if not defining it meant it stayed good, then I was going to let things be.

Then it was Sunday evening and we both knew that he had to go home. It had been nice having him at the house, but he didn't live here and asking him to stay another night would lead to a place I wasn't sure either of us were ready to go. So I didn't ask him to stay. And he didn't offer. What he did do was remind me that if I needed anything, he was there for me to call.

When I went back in to work on Monday morning, I actually felt better than I had in a while. Now, when I thought about Allen's letter, I could almost see why he'd done it. It still hurt, of course, but there was something different when I thought about it now. I could see what Jasper meant about Allen not wanting me to see him like that. I could understand it on an intellectual level, and for now, that was enough to keep me sane.

It was a typical day at school and I hoped that meant things were going to be typical, normal, from here on out. Sure, there was still the hearing about Allen's trust and figuring out what I was going to do about the insurance money, but I hoped this was the point where things would turn around and my life would start getting back on track.

I didn't know how I could be so stupid.

It took all of an hour after getting home from school for me to see that things weren't going to be normal, maybe not ever again.

Mixed in with the rest of my mail was a plain white envelope with my last name scribbled on it. No address, nothing else.

I should've just thrown it away with the rest of the junk mail. I should've left it alone. I didn't need to open it because I knew it wasn't going to be anything nice. Nothing nice ever came in a relatively blank envelope.

But I opened it anyway.

It was short and to the point, brutal in its content and delivery. I was glad I was sitting down when I started to read it because if I hadn't been, I would've ended up on my ass.

*Allen Lockwood wasn't a good man. He was a liar and a bastard. The world is a better place without him.*

I read it three times, each time hoping that it would somehow say something different. That those horrible words would somehow be changed into something that reflected the man I'd known. Yes, he'd lied to me about being sick and what he'd done had been awful, but as much as his actions pained me, I knew they'd been done out of love. No matter how angry I was at him, I couldn't imagine the world being better off for him having died. He hadn't been perfect, but he'd been a good man.

Who would send a letter like this to someone's widow? It was impossibly cruel.

Once I'd recovered enough to start thinking, the Lockwoods were the first people to pop into my mind. Maybe they thought if I was upset enough, I'd want to get away from any place that reminded me of Allen and I'd either give or sell them the vineyard. After all, the letter hadn't come right away. Allen had been gone for nearly four months. Why else would whoever this was wait so long before sending it?

I didn't have proof though. There was no postage on the envelope, which only meant that it hadn't been mailed. The Lockwoods had enough contacts in St. Helena that delivering a letter

31

wouldn't be a big deal, especially since I wouldn't be around to catch anyone doing it.

If I'd thought it'd do any good, I would've taken it to the police so they could test it for fingerprints or DNA or whatever else they could find with their various toys. I knew, however, that no one would care. It wasn't a threat on my life or even against my property. Nothing that could even be interpreted as intimidation. There was no law against being mean and therefore no reason to run expensive tests.

I could have argued that the person who'd written it could've been involved in the arson, but based on the way I'd been treated during the investigation into Allen's death, I didn't trust the St. Helena Police Department to take anything I said seriously, especially since the lead detectives in both cases were the same. Detective Reed didn't even try to hide his low opinion of me and even the "good cop" of the two, Detective Rheingard, most likely believed that I'd had something to do with either Allen's death or the fire, perhaps even both, but he was at least polite about it.

I wanted to crumple it into a ball and throw it away. Tear it into tiny pieces and burn it. I also wanted to hit something, so I knew that giving in to any impulses I currently had would be a bad idea. I carefully folded the letter and put it back into the envelope. I didn't want it out where I could see it though. It was going to be hard enough to get those words out of my head. I didn't need them coming back to me every time I saw the envelope. I went to the office and tucked the letter into one of the desk drawers where I wouldn't accidentally throw it away. It would be available if I needed it for some reason.

I took a slow breath and counted to ten. I couldn't let this letter get me off track. I had some curriculum to look over to see if I wanted to change books the next year. I also had to go over the schedule Jacques Rohner – the foreman at the vineyard – had sent over. The harvest was approaching fast and, as always, it would be a race between ripening and the frost. Between that and the arson, we'd had to take on extra hands to keep an eye on the crop around the clock. I trusted Jacque implicitly and would never have dreamed of telling him to make changes to the way he did things, but he insisted on having me go over anything that required money or had to do with people being on my property.

I had enough on my mind that I didn't need one more thing to worry about. As I headed into the kitchen to get something out to thaw for dinner, I pushed all thoughts of the letter and its author from my mind. I was pleasantly surprised at how well it worked and I didn't think about the letter again until two days later.

The landline was ringing as soon as I walked into the house Wednesday afternoon. I didn't rush to answer it, assuming it was someone from Allen's family. They were the only ones who called that number anymore. It could've been one of the few former clients I hadn't bothered to contact after the accident, but I didn't really want to talk to them either, so I let it go to the answering machine.

I felt a pang as Allen's voice filled the air.

"You have reached Allen and Shae Lockwood. We're unable to come to the phone at this time. Please leave your name, number and a brief message and we'll get back to you as soon as possible."

It was the same trite greeting that most answering machines or voicemails had, but it made me smile. That was pure Allen, concise and polite, no matter how ordinary something sounded. We'd sometimes joked that if Allen hadn't kept on his uncle's marketing team, he would've sold bottles with just "Red Wine" on the label.

I frowned as a full minute passed after the beep with no one speaking. We'd had sales calls on the house phone, but never an obscene phone call. I wondered if this was going to be the first. I wasn't worried about it though. Most of those perverts did it to get a rise out of people, so they wouldn't get much of anything out of a call like this. Maybe they'd get off thinking about someone listening to it, but that seemed a bit far-fetched.

"Mrs. Lockwood."

The voice was raspy, impossible to tell if it belonged to a male or female. What it did do, however, was make all the hairs on the back of my neck stand up.

"I know you're there."

Another pause, as if waiting for me to admit that I was home and go pick up the phone.

"No matter. I know you're listening."

I shivered, suddenly feeling like someone was watching me.

"Your husband wasn't who you thought he was."

Every muscle in my body tensed. The person who'd written the letter. I knew it had to be the same person. It couldn't be a coincidence.

"He wasn't a good man, and you're not a good woman. People like you deserve whatever you get."

I sank down onto a kitchen chair as I heard the click of the line going dead and the machine stopping its recording. I stared at the machine, half-expecting the phone to ring again, to keep ringing until either I answered or the person on the other end drove me insane.

Maybe that's what they were trying to do, I thought. Drive me crazy. Again, I thought of the Lockwoods. It would work to their advantage if I was nuts. They could have me declared incompetent and step in to "take care of me." The only person who'd stand against them would be my brother. And Jasper. I'd have two people against the experts I knew the Lockwoods could provide.

I frowned as the realization hit me. It couldn't be the Lockwoods. Not because they wouldn't do something like that to me. No, this was exactly the kind of thing I could see either May or her son Marcus hiring someone to do.

If it hadn't been for the fact that Allen was being bad-mouthed alongside me. More than me, actually. May and Gregory would never have allowed their precious Allen to be spoken ill of, not even to try to deceive the authorities into discounting them as suspects. Marcus might've done it, or even Alice. Both of them despised me, but I knew that they had both been jealous of Allen and how happy we'd been together. But, neither one of them would've risked their parents' wrath by talking bad about Allen.

But if it wasn't the Lockwoods, who could it be? Allen hadn't had any enemies. Even the competition in the wine industry had been friendly. And if there had been someone who'd wanted to hurt Allen or tarnish his reputation, why now? Why hadn't they done it while he'd been alive, or right after he'd died? Why four months later?

I shifted uneasily. I knew there were workers stationed around the vineyard keeping an eye on things, and that I had a state-of-the-art alarm system, but I still had the sudden and overwhelming feeling that I wasn't safe in my own house.

Jasper.

I reached for my cell phone, needing to hear his voice. I needed to feel safe and he was the one who did that.

My finger hovered over his name for a moment before I set down the phone. I couldn't call Jasper every time I got a bit spooked. Yes, I felt better when he was here but things were already moving so fast between us. I didn't want to ruin what we had by pushing things even faster.

I gritted my teeth and forced myself to my feet. I could do this by myself. I would do this by myself.

My resolve lasted until the next night when, at nearly midnight, the phone rang again. I'd been up finishing a few papers and could hear the answering machine from where I was sitting.

"I know you don't want to hear this, Mrs.

36

Lockwood, but your precious Allen was a liar and a cheat. He used people and discarded them. Maybe you knew that. Maybe you just turned a blind eye to how he treated people. Or maybe you liked it. Did you? Did you like watching him treat people like shit?"

The voice was still rough, but the longer he or she spoke, the louder they got.

"Did it get you off? Do you fantasize about it? Touching yourself when you think about him walking all over people to get what he wanted?"

I picked up my phone, my hands shaking as the caller kept going. I wanted Jasper with me so badly, but I couldn't do that. There was someone else I could call though. Someone who'd drop everything to help me.

"Shae?" Mitchell's voice was thick with sleep. "What's wrong?"

"I need you to come over." I wrapped my arm around my middle as I began to shake. The machine had finally cut off the call, but the words were still echoing in my head. "Please, Mitchell. I can't stay here alone."

"I'm on my way."

# Chapter 5

Mitchell went with me the next morning when I took the answering machine and the letter to the police station before school. He wasn't as big or formidable as Jasper, but he was my big brother. The same one who'd looked after me all my life. The one who'd made it virtually impossible to date. Even when he was at his most annoying and overprotective, he'd always had my best interest at heart.

Not surprisingly, my favorite detectives took down all the information and promised to look into it even as they were turning away. For a moment, I saw Mitchell's temper flash across his blue-green eyes, and I put a hand on his arm. He collected himself and followed me out, but not without first telling the detectives that if anything happened to me while they were sitting on their asses, he'd make sure they lost their jobs.

While I appreciated the sentiment, I couldn't help but wonder if Mitchell had just made things even more difficult for me with the police. Still, he promised that he'd stay until the cops caught whoever was doing this or the calls stopped, and that made me feel better.

By the end of the week, I was thankful Mitchell had stayed. Friday night, I got another call. He picked up the phone and went off on the person on the other end, or at least he tried to. They hung up as soon as they heard his voice. On Saturday, I met Jasper for lunch and when I got home, there was another letter. Mitchell took that one straight to the police station and spent nearly an hour there making threats about what he would do if something happened to me. He didn't say it, but I got the impression that he'd nearly been arrested.

Still, it was only calls and letters. No one tried to get onto the property and I wasn't even bothered at school or when I was with Jasper. I couldn't really relax though, never sure if the person who was doing this was just biding his or her time before launching an assault away from home.

Mitchell stayed in the guest room, not leaving for work until after I did and returning home early enough so that he was there when I arrived. We ate dinner together and then sat in the living room, watching television until we went to bed. Sometimes he went first, sometimes I did, but either way, he always made sure to do a full check of the house to ensure that everything was locked down.

We didn't talk much, but then again, we'd never really been big talkers anyway. We said what we needed to say and we meant it. No games, no pretending. If we didn't want to talk about something, we said it, and we respected the request.

I liked that about Mitchell, that he didn't try to pressure me for information or tell me what I should do.

Well, at least he didn't try to tell me what to do most of the time. He wasn't happy that Jasper and I talked to each other every night before bed or that I'd gone to lunch with him both Saturday and Sunday. He definitely didn't like that I wasn't trying to hide that what was going on between Jasper and me was more than just one good friend checking in on the other to make sure everything was okay. The only thing that kept Mitchell even slightly mollified was the fact that he knew I hadn't told Jasper about the calls or the letters. I didn't want to worry Jasper or make our time together be about that, and Mitchell liked that I'd come to him. He hadn't said it, but I knew it. When I was with Jasper, though, it was the only time I felt normal again. The calls and letters had taken away what little ground I'd gained since Allen's death.

After the second week of the cops doing nothing, I was only too happy to accept Jasper's invitation to go out to a nice restaurant on Saturday evening. So far, we'd only been to a couple diners that were close to Jasper's practice and his house. This would be the first date we'd gone on that would actually feel like a date. Although neither of us commented on the fact, we both knew that Tra Vigne wasn't a place one typically just took a friend.

In the past four years, Allen and I had come here half a dozen times or so, but it wasn't a place that held such important memories of him that I felt weird going with Jasper. I smiled when I saw the familiar ivy-covered building and the smile widened when Jasper reached down and took my hand. I knew the gossip was already going around about the amount of time the two of us were spending together. We hadn't, however, had any real sort of physical contact in public and I knew the moment we walked into the restaurant with our hands clasped together, it'd get ten times worse.

Allen had been the one most people liked. I'd been the quiet one in the background. People hadn't exactly disliked me, but no one had bothered to really get to know me and I'd always been fine with that. I'd always liked keeping to myself.

The fact that I was on a date with his best friend just four months after his death wasn't going to win me any popularity contests. That my date happened to be Jasper Whitehall, the local boy with the black past, was going to make things worse. I didn't think anyone was going to hate me or anything like that, but I doubted anyone would approve.

I hadn't cared what people had thought of me when I'd moved in with Allen even though the Lockwoods had assured me that everyone would think I was only with him for the money. I didn't know if that was true or not, but I hadn't cared then and I didn't care now. I knew who my friends were and they were the only ones whose opinion mattered. And I knew they'd want me to be happy, no matter who I was with.

"You look lovely this evening," Jasper said, raising our hands and brushing his lips across my knuckles.

"You said that already." I smiled at him.

"And I meant it then as well." He returned the smile, his eyes warm.

It was so easy to walk beside him, to enjoy the feel of his fingers between mine. There was none of the first date jitters or nerves. None of the awkward pauses that came with not knowing what to say. We said what we wanted, when we wanted, and if we didn't have anything to say, we stayed quiet. We were as comfortable in silence as we were talking. It was almost eerie how at ease we were with each other. I'd worried that things would get weird when we were around other people, that the way we were with each other wouldn't work in a natural setting.

It did work though. We were still interested in what the other one had to say, still made each other smile and laugh. Every time our fingers brushed or our eyes met for even just a few seconds, familiar heat flowed through me. It was a pleasant feeling, something that I hadn't realized I'd missed in the last four months. The companionship that was more than just sex.

It was building towards that though. I knew it from the moment he'd taken my hand, even if he hadn't known it. I might not have wanted to ask him to stay at the house for an unknown amount of time because I was worried about things moving too fast, but I wasn't about to give up the physical aspect of our relationship. My stomach twisted. I wanted him.

We held hands as we walked back to Jasper's car, but all of the light, airy feeling that had been between us had shifted, and now it was something heavier, darker. Not dark in a bad way, but rather something more visceral, more primal.

He opened my door and then walked around to the other side of the car. He didn't start the car right away, but rather turned towards me with a guarded expression on his face.

"What's wrong?" I asked, immediately concerned.

His eyes darkened. "You didn't hear them?"

"Which ones?" I asked wryly, trying to suppress a smile. "The old women in the corner who were talking too loudly about how back in their day, a widow would wear black for a certain period of mourning? Or the man talking to the hostess about how long he thought it had been after Allen's death before the two of us started sleeping together?"

His face tightened and his hands flexed. "I should've known better. We should've gone somewhere else."

"It's okay." I put my hand over his. "I knew what it would be like. The people here love a good scandal, but they'll forget about it soon enough."

"Is that what we are?" he asked. "A forgettable scandal?"

I tilted my head, unable to read him. "Do you think of us that way?"

He looked away from me. "I think I'm your late husband's best friend and I'm your friend. The person you call when you need something from someone." He looked down at his hands. "Whatever you need."

Something twisted inside me. "Is that what you think?" My voice nearly shook with the myriad emotions I was feeling. "Do you think I just call you when I need something? When there's some problem I can't fix on my own?" My tone hardened. "Or maybe when I want to get laid? Is that really the kind of person you think I am?"

His head whipped around, his eyes wide. "No! Shae, no!"

"Then what, Jasper? Am I using you?"

That's when I saw it. It was only there for a moment, and then gone, but I recognized it. If I hadn't known him so well, I wouldn't have caught it.

"You do, don't you?" I asked, not even trying to keep the shock out of my voice. "You think I'm using you. Fuck, Jasper! How could you think that?!" I started to reach for the door.

He leaned across me and put his hand over mine. I turned my head and his face was just inches from mine. His eyes were that deep smoky gray that usually made everything inside me melt, but at the moment, they made me want to cry. How could he think I was using him?

"I told you I would be here for you, Shae, be anything for you, and I meant it." His voice was soft. "I'm not asking you for anything."

"Then what the hell was that all about?" I asked.

He reached out with his free hand and tucked a strand of hair behind my ear. "I'm sorry. Don't even worry about it."

"But I do worry," I said. I put my hand on his cheek. "I don't know what this is between us, but I'm

45

not using you, Jasper." I leaned forward to press my lips against his. It was a chaste kiss, but a firm one. "I appreciate everything you've done for me, but I don't sleep with people just because they're nice to me."

That got a hint of a smile. "That's good to know."

"What about you?" I asked, my thumb teasing at the corner of his mouth.

"What about me?"

"Should I be worried that you're using me?"

The look of horror on his face would've made me laugh if the air between us hadn't been so thick with tension.

His expression softened as he released my wrist and used both of his hands to cup my face. "Shae, I could never do that to you." His eyes met mine. "I swear, I will never ask for anything you aren't willing to give."

My stomach tightened. I'd been honest when I told Jasper that I didn't know what we were, but I did know one thing for sure.

I wanted him.

Now.

# Chapter 6

I'd been to Jasper's house a couple times before, but always with Allen. Most of our time together had been spent at the vineyard, but every once in a while we'd come to the little place that Jasper had bought for himself when he'd started working with his father.

It felt different this time as Jasper held the door open for me.

I'd always liked his house. It was a fraction of the size of the vineyard, with everything on one floor and a decent-sized yard. Two bedrooms, a single bath, a nice kitchen and a living room big enough to have some friends over. It didn't look like a typical bachelor pad, but it wasn't overly decorated either. Jasper's tastes were simple and nice. I'd always felt at home here.

I didn't pay attention to any of that as I kicked off my shoes the instant I crossed the doorway. The only thing I cared about was the man standing in front of me and getting us both naked as quickly as possible.

We were a tangle of limbs and clothing, of teeth

and tongues, not wanting to stop touching each other even just to undress. Somehow, we managed to get back to his bedroom, leaving a trail of clothes behind us. When Jasper finally pulled his mouth away, we were both gasping for air and completely naked.

His eyes ran over me, making my already overheated skin burn even hotter. I watched him watching me, his face an open book to everything he was feeling.

Desire.

Lust.

Awe.

And something deeper that told me he cared about me more than I'd realized.

"You're so fucking beautiful." His voice was rough.

"So are you." I did my own perusal, letting my gaze run across his handsome face to his broad shoulders. Down his muscular torso to his narrow waist. My eyes followed the thin trail of dark curls from his bellybutton to where his cock was waiting, thick and hard.

My stomach tightened and I reached out, giving him a gentle shove back towards the bed. His eyes widened slightly in surprise, but he let me push him onto the bed. I climbed up next to him, settling on my knees next to his waist. He moaned when my fingers closed around his dick and I smiled. I loved that I could make this strong, gorgeous man make those kinds of sounds.

The skin was so soft, the rest of him impossibly

hard. If I'd been in the mood for something slow and drawn out, I would've spent as much time as possible exploring every inch of his body, but I didn't want slow right now. Maybe later. What I did want, however, was to taste him.

I gripped the base of him and ran my tongue up his shaft. He swore as I licked him, tasted him, felt every inch of him pulsing against my tongue. He was so different than Allen and I wasn't sure why that surprised me. He'd felt different inside me and now I could taste it as well. Not better. Not worse. Just different.

"Shae..." My name was barely a whisper.

I leaned down, my hair brushing against his thighs as I took him into my mouth. He made a half-strangled sound and I saw his hand fist against his thigh. I let more of him inside and used my hand around the thickest part of him, knowing I'd never be able to take him all. His hips jerked slightly and I knew he was fighting the urge to move, to thrust deep into my mouth.

Something low and primal inside me throbbed at the thought of him doing just that, of him using my mouth for his own pleasure, but again, that was something that was going to have to wait. As much as I was enjoying the sensation of him sliding over my tongue, enjoying the sounds he was making, I wanted him inside me more.

I needed him inside me.

I raised my head, my eyes meeting his as the last inch slipped from between my lips. Keeping our gazes locked, I swung one leg over him so that I was straddling his waist, his cock between my thighs.

I put one hand on his stomach, smiling at the way the muscles twitched beneath my palms. The other hand reached beneath me to hold him steady as I lowered myself onto him. His hands went to my hips, fingers digging into the flesh as I took the first inch of him inside me.

My eyelids fluttered even at the slight stretch. The other two times we'd done this, he'd used his fingers and mouth on me until I came, allowing him relatively easy passage. This time, however, I was wet, but not prepared any other way.

This was going to be intense.

I put both hands on his stomach and let myself slide down until I was resting on his lap.

"Fuck," I whispered as I squeezed my eyes shut. Every muscle in my body was trembling as if he wasn't simply stretching me, filling me, in one place, but in every cell.

I'd never felt anything like it, not even with Allen. He'd always treated me like something precious. Like I'd break if he wasn't careful. Now, I felt like I was going to shatter with the slightest touch, but I wanted more, wanted to move.

I shifted my weight, drawing a groan from Jasper. My own moan joined his as his cock rubbed against my walls, sending a new ripple of sensation through me. I opened my eyes and found Jasper watching me, the intensity of his gaze sending a shiver through me.

I lifted myself up until just the tip of him was still inside and then dropped down, sending a burst of almost painful pleasure through me as he went deeper than before. One of the hands on my hip moved up to my breast, squeezing for a moment before his fingers started manipulating my nipple, pulling and rolling even as I repeated my rise and fall.

Neither one of us spoke as I rode him. Only the sounds of flesh against flesh mingled with our harsh breathing. I could feel the pressure inside me building, but just before I reached it, he sat up, his mouth immediately covering mine. One arm slid around my waist, holding me in place as he began to move us both. I whimpered as his tongue delved into my mouth, sliding against mine. The base of his cock was rubbing directly on my clit now and every shallow thrust created new, wonderful friction.

His lips moved across my jaw, teeth scraping against my skin before his tongue soothed it. He leaned me back, his arm stretched along my spine. He fastened his lips around one hard nipple. The suction was immediate and hard, sending a jolt of near-pain straight down. Then his teeth began to worry the sensitive flesh and I squirmed, wanting the sweet torture to stop. To never stop.

I gasped his name, digging my nails into his shoulders as he bit down. My entire body tensed, trapping him inside me even as my pussy squeezed tight around him. He buried his hand in my hair as I came, mouth still sucking hard on my breast until I was certain I would explode.

Then, suddenly, he was flipping us over, pinning my body under his. His fist tightened in my hair as he drove into me, forcing one orgasm into a second and then a third as he managed to hit that spot inside me with unerring accuracy. My nipple throbbed when he released it and I raked my nails down his back, gripping his firm ass even as he began to suck on my neck. He was going to leave a mark, I knew, but I didn't care about that at the moment. All I cared about was that he never stopped.

"More." I raised my hips to meet his, driving him deep enough to make me cry out. I felt his slight hesitation and clutched him tighter. "Don't stop."

He growled and wrapped one hand around my calf, pulling my leg high and opening me even wider. My eyes closed and my head fell back. My hand clutched him, holding on as he rode my body as thoroughly as I'd been riding his. I couldn't move, couldn't do anything but try to absorb everything I was feeling until it finally burst over me like a blinding light.

I cried out his name as I came again and I felt his entire body shudder. He thrust into me again, taking me deep and hard as he came. He collapsed onto me even as his cock pulsed and emptied inside of me. He wrapped his arms around me, shifting us so that he didn't crush me, but still stayed inside me, our bodies joined. He pressed his lips against my forehead and I turned my face against his chest, feeling the racing beat of his heart against my mouth.

I wasn't ready to say that this was love, but a part of me knew that if it wasn't already, it would be soon. The thought was both terrifying and comforting, but I knew I didn't have to dwell on it now. For the time being, it was enough for us to just be together and care about each other.

# Chapter 7

I'd fully expected to wake up the next morning and find Jasper up and doing something. Making breakfast. Taking a shower.

I certainly never expected to be woken up by the feel of his mouth between my legs, licking and sucking until I came hard against his mouth. Remembering what I'd been thinking the day before when I'd gone down on him, I was only too happy to reciprocate, taking him into my mouth until he called out my name. I swallowed every last drop and then crawled back up his body to snuggle against his side. We'd had sex two more times during the night. Once drawn-out and almost lazy, our bodies moving with and against each other as our foreheads rested together. The other hard and quick. He'd taken me from behind, his hand in my hair, his body curved over my back. His free hand between my legs, keeping constant pressure and friction on my clit until I was nearly in tears.

I could feel it all now. My entire body ached. His mouth on my clit and pussy had almost been too much for the overstimulated flesh and I wasn't even sure I'd be able to shower without feeling every drop of water with excruciating intensity.

I didn't want to shower yet though. I just wanted to lay here in Jasper's arms and pretend that this was the way things were, that there wasn't anything out in the world that would try to keep us apart. I wanted the simplicity of it even though I knew I could never have it.

I let myself pretend for a few more minutes before sitting up with a sigh.

"You have to go." Jasper gave me a soft smile.

"I do." I reached down and traced his bottom lip with my finger. "But I don't regret any of this."

He caught my hand between his and pressed my knuckles to his lips. "Me either." His breath was hot against my skin and my stomach tightened.

How could I want him again?

I didn't take the time to stop and analyze it because I knew if I did, I'd act on it, and I'd never leave. As tempting as that idea was, I knew I had to go. I had work to do at home and if Mitchell wasn't worried already, he would be soon. I'd left him a note saying that I was going out and that my phone would be off, but that didn't mean he wouldn't be concerned.

I leaned down and lightly kissed Jasper before climbing out of the bed and heading for the bathroom. I didn't have clean clothes to wear home, but I definitely wasn't going to go like this. One glance in the mirror confirmed that a shower was a good decision. My hair was a wild, tangled mess, my lips swollen. I flushed at the dark marks Jasper's mouth had left on my breasts and neck. I was suddenly glad the weather was cool enough for me to wear high-necked shirts, otherwise, I'd have some awkward questions ahead of me.

Then there were the parts that I couldn't see, but I felt. The stickiness on my thighs from our combined fluids, the slight change in the way I was walking to put less pressure and friction on my sensitive skin. My pussy throbbing in time with my heart and I knew that I was going to be feeling all of this for the rest of the day.

When I came out of the shower twenty minutes later, I felt much cleaner, but still sore. I wrapped the towel tightly around me as I went back into the bathroom. Jasper was standing by his dresser, naked, his back to me. I flushed when I saw the long, red scratches down his back and even on his ass.

Shit. I hadn't realized I'd done that.

"Do you want something to wear home?" He half-turned, completely unembarrassed by the fact that he was still naked. He held up a pair of sweatpants and a t-shirt. "They'll be huge on you, but at least they're clean."

"Thank you." I reached for him and felt my face heat again when his eyes automatically went to the mark he'd left on my neck.

He reached out and brushed his finger over it. "I'm sorry. I got a bit carried away."

I stared at him for a moment and then laughed. "Seriously?"

"What?" He gave me a puzzled look.

I dropped the towel and gestured for him to look lower. I saw the desire in his eyes first, followed by surprise. I had at least four more hickeys and two bite marks on my breasts.

"Fuck, Shae. I'm so sorry. I didn't mean to do that." He started to reach for me, then dropped his hand, his cheeks flushed.

I shook my head and laughed again. "No need to apologize, Jasper. I enjoyed your...attention." My eyes slid to the mirror where I could see the reflection of his back. "Besides, I'm pretty sure I gave as good as I got."

"What?"

"Look over your shoulder."

He did, eyes widening as he saw the scratches I'd made.

"You can't see all of them," I said, my cheeks burning. "But when you get in the shower, I'm sure you'll feel them."

He looked down at me, a smile curving his lips. "I guess we're even then."

"I wouldn't go that far," I said as I took a step towards him. We weren't touching, but I could feel the heat from his body. "Next time, it's my turn to bite."

It was nearly noon by the time Jasper finally dropped me off at my place, and as I'd suspected he would be, Mitchell was waiting on the porch. I leaned over and kissed Jasper's cheek.

"I'll talk to you later, okay?"

I got out of the car before he could ask anything about my brother. I could feel his eyes on me, but he didn't get out of the car. Yet another thing that I loved about Jasper. He knew me well enough to know when I was posturing and when I was serious. And I'd been serious about not wanting him and Mitchell to get into it.

"What the hell, Shae?" Mitchell burst out as Jasper drove away.

"I left you a note," I said mildly as I walked past my brother and into my house. "I said I didn't know when I'd be home and not to wait up."

"Yeah," he said as he followed me upstairs. "But you didn't say you'd be out fucking Jasper Whitehall all night."

I turned, clutching my clothes to my chest to keep myself from slapping my brother. "Not that it's any of your business, but Jasper and I care about each other. It's called a relationship, Mitchell."

His eyes flashed. "You can't be serious. *Him?* Allen's only been gone for four months. What's gotten into you?"

I took a slow breath and then let it out just as slowly. "I'm an adult, Mitchell. I know you care about me, but I'm twenty-six years-old and have been on my own since I left for college. I'm a widow, not some naïve little college girl about to go off on her own for the first time."

"You'll always be my little sister," he said gruffly.

"I know." My voice softened. "But it's my life. My choice."

I went downstairs without waiting for a response. I tossed my dirty clothes into the basket near the washer and then went back into the living room. Mitchell was still there, scowling, but at least he didn't argue when I walked in. I picked up the mail sitting on the table and began to go through it, wanting to give Mitchell the chance to finish absorbing what I'd said before I spoke to him again.

I immediately tensed as I saw the envelope. Blank except for my name. This time, my first name was also included. My fingers were shaking so badly that I could barely tear the flap open.

It wasn't a letter this time. It was a picture.

"Shae, what's wrong?"

Mitchell's voice sounded like it was coming from a far-off distance.

I couldn't stop staring at the picture. It was Allen in a UCLA sweatshirt. He was young, his face youthful and smiling. Tawny hair, hazel eyes. Strong jaw. Nose that was a bit too long. It was Allen. My Allen.

Except I wasn't the woman standing next to him. No, I amended, a girl, not a woman. She might've been eighteen or nineteen, but she had the kind of build and features that would have people thinking of her as a girl for years to come. Her eyes were a dark brown, her hair long and curly, the color

58

of cocoa. She was tiny, barely coming to Allen's shoulder.

His arm was around her in a possessive gesture I recognized all too well.

I flipped the picture over, but there wasn't anything written on it. No note in the envelope. Only the picture of my late husband and some woman I'd never seen before.

Who was she? Why had I been sent her picture?

A thousand things flew through my mine, but before I could get a grip on any of them, someone knocked on the door.

I walked over and opened it to find Jasper standing there, my purse in his hand. I hadn't even realized I'd left it. He took one look at my face and his expression darkened.

"What's wrong?"

"Don't worry about it, Whitehall," Mitchell growled from over my shoulder. "I can take care of my sister."

Jasper's eyes narrowed. "What do you mean take care of her?" He looked at me. "Shae, what's going on? Why is Mitchell here? And why do you look like you've just seen a ghost?"

I barked out a nervous laugh. A ghost. Yeah, that was pretty close to the truth. I held out the picture.

"Shae," Mitchell warned.

"Didn't you say you had somewhere you were supposed to be today?" I asked, shooting my brother a sharp glance.

He glared at me and then at Jasper before turning back to me again. "I do." He stomped past us both and climbed into his truck, peeling out of the driveway.

"What's going on, Shae?" Jasper glanced down at the picture. "Why do you have a picture of Aime Vargas?"

Oh. She had a name. Of course she did.

I walked over to the porch swing and sunk down on it. "Who is she?" I asked.

Jasper came over and sat next to me. "She and Allen dated during his junior year of college and he broke it off at the end of the year. She didn't come back to UCLA the next year. Where did you get this?"

"In the mail," I said, holding up the envelope.

"I don't understand."

I nodded. "I know you don't." After taking a moment to collect myself, I told him the whole story, starting with the first letter I received. As I spoke, the expression on his face kept growing darker. When I finally stopped, he was silent for nearly a whole minute.

"Why didn't you call me?"

I looked down at my hands. "Because I kept calling you for everything. It wasn't a big deal for Mitchell to come."

"I wouldn't have minded." The words were mild, but I could hear the edge to them.

"I know."

"Then why." He reached out and cupped my chin, turning my head so I had to look at him. "Why wouldn't you call me or at least tell me about what happened? We were together all night and you never once thought to bring this up? I told you I wanted to take care of you."

I forced myself to meet his eyes. "Because I felt like asking you to stay here for an unknown amount of time would be moving too fast and I didn't want to scare you off."

"Shae, you could never do that," he said sincerely.

"That was only part of it," I said, taking a deep breath. "I also didn't want you to feel like I only came to you when I needed something."

Understanding dawned on his face. "That's why you were so upset about what I said after dinner."

I nodded.

He took my hand and squeezed it. "Well, now that I know, what can I do to help?"

I squeezed his hand back and some of the tension went out of me. He was here. He was going to help me, even if it was only by sitting by my side. Before I could think of anything that I needed him to do, a car pulled up the driveway.

We stood and watched as it parked and the driver's side door opened. A tiny woman got out and started walking towards us.

"Shit," Jasper breathed. "Aime."

I didn't need him to tell me her name again. She didn't look much different than she did in the photo. What was different, however, was the little girl behind her. Tiny, with light brown curls and dark eyes, she looked a lot like Aime.

My blood turned to ice. I knew what she was going to say, but I stayed where I was and let her finish coming to me.

"Shae Lockwood?" Aime stopped a few feet away from me.

"Yes." I crossed my arms. "Aime Vargas?"

Her eyes widened a bit in surprise, then flicked to Jasper. She recognized him, I was sure of it, but she didn't say a word to him. Instead, she focused all of her attention on me.

"I'm Aime." She reached behind her and pulled the girl up beside her. "This is Jenny. She's Allen's daughter and we're here for what's hers."

# Chapter 8

For the first couple weeks after Allen had died, there were times when it had all felt so surreal that I thought I could convince myself that it was all just a bad dream. A few times I'd even had dreams that none of this had happened, that Allen hadn't died right in front of me. That we were still married, had a family.

This was another one of those moments.

It had to be a dream. A nightmare, actually.

There was no way I could be standing here, next to my dead husband's best friend who I was now dating, listening to said late husband's ex-girlfriend say that he had a daughter.

Allen didn't have kids.

We'd wanted kids and had planned to start trying just before he'd died. Or, at least, that's what I'd thought we were trying to do. Then I'd gotten the letter letting me know he'd been so sick. Why had he led me to believe we could have children together when he knew we never would?

Or that he already had a kid.

A daughter.

One with big dark eyes and light brown curls.

One who was standing behind her mother and looking for all the world like she didn't want to be there.

It was the look on the girl's face more than anything that broke me out of the strange trance that the words had put me under.

"What?"

My response was far from elegant or even particularly unique or insightful, but it was a question at least.

Aime smirked at me and the surreal feeling disappeared under annoyance. Even if she hadn't been Allen's ex, I wouldn't have liked her.

"Allen and I were together for a year," Aime said. "Jenny's his daughter."

I looked at Jasper, waiting for him to tell me that she was lying, that Allen didn't have a child, but Jasper didn't say a word. He was staring at the little girl. I wondered for a moment if he was trying to see the same thing I'd tried to see when I looked at her. But it was pointless to try to see Allen in the girl. She looked too much like her mother.

A mother who was totally gorgeous.

I was suddenly aware of the fact that I was still wearing Jasper's t-shirt and sweatpants.

"Jasper." I reached out and touched his arm.

He looked down at me.

"Jasper Whitehall." Aime's smirk widened into a smile. "I thought that was you. I can't believe it's been ten years."

"Aime." Jasper didn't look at her.

"Well, since you know that Allen and I were...together, then you know that Jenny is Allen's daughter."

I swallowed hard, my fingers tightening around his arm. "Is that true, Jasper? Did you know about her?" My stomach twisted. "Did Allen know?"

"No." Jasper's tone was firm. "Allen and Aime dated. There was no baby." He turned towards Aime, his eyes flashing. "She looks a bit young to have been Allen's child because I definitely know that he met Shae three months after you two broke up and he never cheated."

I had a feeling if Jenny hadn't been there, Jasper's word choice would've been a lot less polite.

Aime's mouth flattened. "You don't know shit."

I winced, then glared at her. I wanted to tell her to watch her mouth, but Jenny wasn't my daughter.

She was my step-daughter?

What would she be to me if Allen was her father? Nothing because he was dead? Would that even matter?

My head throbbed and I knew I had a massive headache coming on. My eyes dropped to the girl as she practically hid behind her mother.

"How old are you?" I figured I was more likely to get a truthful answer out of the kid. Some kids might have been natural liars, but my gut said she was going to tell me the truth.

"Eight and a half."

Her voice was barely a whisper.

"So you would've gotten pregnant..." I let my voice trail off.

65

"A little over nine years ago." Aime crossed her arms and raised her eyebrows. "When Jasper here will tell you that I was dating Allen."

One look at Jasper's face was enough to tell me that she was being truthful about the timeline at least.

"You might've been with him, but that doesn't mean Jenny's his daughter," Jasper said. He reached down and took my hand, cold fingers grasping mine. I wasn't even sure if he was doing it for my comfort or his.

"His name's on the birth certificate."

I was suddenly glad Jasper was holding my hand because if he hadn't been, I most likely would've tried to slap the smug expression off her face, even with Jenny there.

"That doesn't mean sh...anything," Jasper said, his gaze darting down to the girl and then back up again. "You could've put anyone's name down on that. Could've been mine even though we both know I turned you down flat."

My fingers twitched in his hand as Aime's cheeks flushed red. She looked down at our hands and then shook her head.

"Are you kidding me? You were Allen's best friend and now you're fucking his wife?" She rolled her eyes when she saw me look at Jenny. "Trust me, not the first time the kid's heard that word."

"This has nothing to do with us," Jasper said. "This is about you claiming to have had Allen's child."

"She's Allen's," Aime said. "We both know it."

"All I know is that you're saying she is and your proof is that my late husband's name's on the birth certificate and that you'd been sleeping with him during the time she'd been conceived." My voice was stronger than I'd expected.

"Oh, honey, you don't wanna play chicken with me," she said. "You'll end up smeared all over the road."

She intended to intimidate me, and I supposed if I'd met her back when Allen and I had first started dating, it might've worked, but I'd spent far too much time with the Lockwoods looking down at me, trying to do the same thing she was trying. If May Lockwood couldn't scare me away from her son, there was no way some blast from Allen's past would manage to freak me out with a single comment.

"I don't know you," I said. "And you don't know me, but let me tell you this. You can't scare me into giving you what you want."

One side of Aime's mouth twisted up into a smile. "Oh, it's not giving me what I want. It's giving my daughter what she deserves."

"Why now?" Jasper asked suddenly. Aime and I both looked at him. "Why did it take you nine years to come here with her? Why didn't you tell Allen when you first found out?"

That was an excellent point, I realized. I hadn't even thought about that. I looked expectantly at Aime.

"You're the ones who said Allen didn't know." She patted the little girl's head. "What would you say if I told you that Allen knew? That he'd known since

67

before Jenny was born, but that he didn't want to be tied down with a family. That he'd been paying me all this time and the reason I came forward now is because the money's gone."

I was going to throw up.

It couldn't be true. Her claim was bad enough, but to say that Allen had known, that he'd been paying her all this time and lying about it. It was too much.

"You will give me what I want," she said, taking a step forward. Her dark eyes were flashing angrily. "And if I have to, I'll take you to court for it. I'll make sure the whole world knows what a bastard Allen Lockwood was and what a bitch he married."

"That's enough." Jasper stepped in front of me, using his grip on my hand to move me behind him. "You need to leave. Now."

I'd known he was a big man, but I'd never really seen him use his size before. Now, it was a presence, a presence that stood between myself and Aime.

"I'll leave," Aime said. "But this isn't the end of it."

Jasper didn't move until Aime's car disappeared down the driveway. Only then did he turn towards me, his arms automatically going around me, pulling me against his broad chest.

My thoughts were chaotic, my head spinning, and I let myself relax into his embrace, let him hold me. How could this be happening? Just one more thing on top of everything else that was going on.

Aime had sent the threats. Even if the last picture hadn't been of her and Allen, I would've guessed that she'd been the culprit. She wasn't just pissed at Allen, but at me too. I knew why. He'd broken up with her and less than six months later, he'd met me. Of course she had a right to be angry, especially since she'd been pregnant.

But none of that meant that Allen had known about Jenny.

He couldn't have known. Not like that. The man I'd known couldn't have just walked away from his daughter, no matter what Aime said. If he'd known about Jenny, he would've provided for her, but not hidden her. He would've told me about her, would have shared custody. He would've put her into his will.

He would have told me.

Like he would've told me that he was sick? That he was dying?

Allen had lied to me about that. Had killed himself.

What if he'd lied to me about this too?

# Chapter 9

"Do you think he knew?" My question was muffled against his chest. "Tell me the truth, Jas. Do you think he knew about his daughter?"

He gripped my shoulders and pulled me back so that we could look at each other. "No, Shae." There was no doubt in his eyes. "If Allen had known, he never would've let Aime have custody. He would've fought tooth and nail to get custody of his daughter. He would have told you. Would have wanted her to meet you."

"Are you sure?" I didn't like how small and unsure I sounded, but I wasn't embarrassed by it. Jasper was the one person I didn't have to hide from, didn't have to be strong for.

He cupped my chin, his thumb brushing over my bottom lip. "Why wouldn't he want his daughter to meet you?"

I looked away. "I don't know..."

"Hey." His fingers tightened on my chin. "Look at me." His voice was low, firm.

Reluctantly, I did as he said.

"You are a kind, caring woman, Shae. An amazing woman. Any man would be grateful to have you meet their child, to be a mother to their daughter." He ran his fingers down the side of my face. "Allen was like a brother to me and I knew how he felt about you. If he'd had a daughter, he would've told me. Then he would've told you when he knew things were going to be serious, which was about two days after he met you."

I leaned into his touch and closed my eyes. "I know that. I mean, I know it in my head, but after the letter..."

"You aren't sure what to believe." He finished my sentence.

I sighed and opened my eyes. "How do you manage to know what I'm thinking?"

He smiled as he leaned down and kissed the tip of my nose. "Because I've spent the last eight years watching you." He groaned a moment later and chuckled. "That sounded really creepy, didn't it?"

I laughed, some of the tension easing. "A little bit."

He raised an eyebrow and slid his hands down my arms. "Any chance I could do something to make you forget about it?"

"Well." I pretended to consider the question. "My brother's being an ass. My late husband's ex-girlfriend just announced that they had a child together. What I really want is to not have to think about any of it."

He looked down at me for a moment and then took a step back. I gave him a puzzled look as he

72

took my hand and led me off the porch.

"Where are we going?" I'd been thinking my request was pretty obvious. Maybe I should've just told him that I wanted him to take me into the house and fuck me until I couldn't remember my own name.

"Let's take a walk."

"A walk?" I echoed.

He smiled, his eyes shining. "Yes, Shae. Let's take a walk. Show me how well the vineyard's doing. Let's talk grapes and wine."

I let him lead me towards the vines and we began to walk down the rows. We moved slowly, taking our time. It was a perfect October afternoon. The sun was out, but there were enough clouds to give us some shade. The breeze was cool but not too cold and carried just a hint of autumn. The scent of the grapes was heavy on the air, a rich, heady smell that reminded me of the prior years when I'd take walks like this with Allen.

"How's the harvest looking?" Jasper asked, finally breaking the silence.

"Good." I squinted up at the sun, enjoying the warmth. "Jacques says we didn't lose enough in the fire to make much of a dent in our production. If the frost can stay away just a bit longer, everything should go smoothly."

"Have you been watching the weather reports? It looks like things are going to be going your way."

I laughed and shook my head.

"What?" Jasper gave me a confused look.

"Are you seriously talking to me about the

weather?"

He laughed too. "I suppose I am."

"Do you really want to talk about the grapes and frost?"

He stopped so suddenly that I took an extra step before I realized he wasn't beside me anymore. Then he was pulling me towards him hard enough that I automatically put my hands out as I collided with his chest.

"No." His voice was low, husky. "I don't want to talk."

"Then what do you want?" I asked softly.

"You, Shae." He bent his head towards me. "Always you."

The moment his mouth touched mine, everything else ceased to matter. His tongue slipped between my lips as one hand cupped the back of my head. The other hand pressed against the small of my back, burning through the soft cotton of my shirt. *His* shirt.

"Shae," he murmured my name as he broke the kiss. He rested his forehead against mine as he pushed one hand through my hair. He sighed. "I'm sorry."

"You apologize too much," I said. "Why this time?" I slid my hands down his chest and around his waist. I loved the strength I felt there, the way his muscles were firm and tight under my palms.

"I said we were going to take a walk so you could forget about everything else and I go and kiss you."

"I didn't mind." I smiled at him and brushed my lips across his.

"You don't get it, Shae." He closed his eyes. "When I'm with you, it's like...I've been wanting to touch you, hold you, and now that I can..." He opened his eyes and pulled me even more tightly against him. "I want you so badly and I don't want to scare you away."

I dropped my hands lower until they were on his ass. He sucked in a breath.

"I'm not going anywhere, Jas. And I want you too." My entire body throbbed with how much I wanted him.

"Back to the house?" he asked, a hopeful note in his voice.

I shook my head. Allen and I had sometimes kissed when we'd taken our walks, but some part of me had always wanted to do something a bit more adventurous. What was the point of having all of this if I couldn't enjoy it, right?

"Here."

His eyebrows went up, eyes widening. "Here?"

I nodded and leaned forward, taking his bottom lip between my teeth. I pulled it into my mouth, sucking and nipping until he groaned. I let it go.

"Here," I whispered. "Now."

He pulled his shirt off and I made a soft sound in the back of my throat. He chuckled, the kind of rich, very male sound that made me instantly wet.

"What's so funny?" I asked as he spread his shirt out on the ground.

"That sound you made when I took my shirt off." He grinned at me, a sheepish expression on his face.

I flushed, looking down. His hand cupped my

chin and raised my head so our eyes could meet.

"I'm sorry I laughed," he said seriously. "It's just..." He seemed to struggle to find the words. "I never thought I'd hear you ever make a sound like that about me."

I put my hand on his chest, feeling the steady beat of his heart under my palm. When I ran my other hand across his chest, down to his abs, his pulse skipped and I smiled.

"What?" he asked.

"Your heart." I leaned forward and pressed my lips to his chest. When I opened my mouth and flicked out my tongue, I felt him catch his breath. I looked up and my chest tightened at what I saw in his face. "I love the way your body reacts to me." I flushed as I said it, but when I saw the pure joy that filled his eyes, I knew a little embarrassment was worth it.

He dropped to his knees in front of me and I put my hand on his head, running my fingers through his soft, thick hair. He put his hands on my hips, using his thumbs to bunch up the shirt until a thin strip of skin was exposed.

"Do you know how much I love seeing you in my clothes?" He pressed his lips against my stomach.

"And here I'd been feeling frumpy compared to Aime."

He gave me a sharp look. "She doesn't even compare to you." He kissed my stomach again and then hooked his fingers under the waistband of my pants.

My fingers tightened in his hair as he slid the

sweats down to my knees. The shirt fell down, covering me to the tops of my thighs, but he didn't let that deter him. He ducked his head under the shirt, his hands holding onto my hips as he maneuvered himself between my legs. I gasped as his tongue parted my folds and I grabbed onto his shoulders. My head fell forward, eyes fluttering shut as waves of pleasure washed over me.

When his tongue found my still-sensitive clit, I cried out, knees buckling, but he held me up, somehow managing to shift me so that I was leaning almost completely on him. A finger slipped inside me, twisting and curling until he hit that spot and I cried out.

Even while I was coming, he eased me down onto his shirt. I barely registered the sound of a zipper and then he was over me and inside me. I cried out again as he stretched me wide, the myriad sensations pushing me into another climax before the first had even finished. His mouth covered mine, swallowing every sound as he thrust into me. His strokes were slow and deep, filling me with each one until I was no longer sure which body was his and which was mine. I'd experienced this sort of closeness with Allen only a few times and never this intense. It was almost overwhelming.

My nails dug into Jasper's arms as my teeth scraped over his lip. He moaned, his mouth leaving mine to bite his way down my neck. I moved my hands to his back, sliding them down to his ass. I pushed at the jeans that were only half-way down, nails scratching at his already marked skin. I wanted to mark him more, I realized, and I wanted him to mark me. This was the part of the weekend I wanted to think about whenever I got dressed, whenever I looked in the mirror.

"Please, Jas," I begged as he licked and bit at my throat. "I'm so close."

I could feel it coming, that precipice that could take me away from here to a place where it was just him and me. Nothing else. No problems. No one telling us we shouldn't be together. We just were.

"Come for me, baby."

His voice was low in my ear.

"You're so beautiful when you come."

He shifted his hips, rubbing against my clit with just the right amount of pressure and then I was flying. The world exploded around me in white and I called out his name. He moved inside me even as I clamped down around him and I heard him swear. Heard him say my name. A shudder ran through him and he came.

Slowly, I became aware of the world around me again. The buzz of insects. The thick smell of grapes mingled with the scent of sex. The weight and heat of Jasper's body wrapped around me. The feel of his cum on the insides of my thighs. The hard ground under his shirt.

He brushed some hair back from my face as he leaned over me, propped on one arm. His face was concerned. "I wasn't too rough, was I?"

"No." I smiled and reached up to put my hand on his cheek. "It was perfect. I like variety."

He laughed, but there was a hint of something

sad to the sound. "After eight years with the same person, I suppose anything different would be variety."

"That's not what I meant." I lifted my head to kiss him. "I like all the ways you have sex with me. Slow. Fast. Hard. Soft." I sighed.

"What's wrong then?" he asked.

"I love being with you. Spending time with you. Having sex with you."

"Okay?" He looked confused.

"But everyone keeps saying that it's too soon." I rolled onto my side so we could be face-to-face.

"Do you feel like it's too fast?"

I could hear the hesitation in his voice and knew that if I said yes, he'd back off. But I didn't want him to back off. I didn't want to take this slow, I realized.

"Fuck it."

His eyes widened.

"It's not like you're some random stranger, Jas. I've known you for years. It's only this part of things that's new. Do you think we're going too fast?"

He shook his head. "I've wanted this for a long time," he admitted. "I'll go whatever speed you want as long as I can be with you."

I smiled. "Good, because I'm tired of listening to what other people say and I'm tired of living in the past." I took a deep breath. "Move in with me."

# Chapter 10

*I'm just glad Mom's not here to see this. She would've been ashamed of you.*

It had been five days since Mitchell had left and his words still echoed in my head, no matter how hard I tried to get them out.

Jasper had stayed through Sunday evening, the day I'd asked him to move in with me and we'd gone over the logistics of things. When the best time would be for him to move in. What he was going to bring and where those things were going to go. If I thought I'd be able to clean out the last of Allen's things or if I'd need help.

The one thing I hadn't considered was how to tell my brother. I'd have been lying if I'd said it had slipped my mind though. It was more like I'd purposefully pushed the idea to the back of the list. I'd known that Mitchell wouldn't like it and I just hadn't wanted to deal.

Instead, I'd focused on the other things. Where I was going to donate the last of Allen's clothes. Whether or not Jasper and I should switch the bedrooms around so that we weren't using the same room Allen and I had occupied for the last few years. How many pictures would be too many to leave up and out.

As we'd talked, I'd realized the best part of having fallen for my late husband's best friend. Jasper missed Allen as much as I did and he understood that I wouldn't want to pretend that the last eight years hadn't happened. He wanted to remember Allen, to talk about the things the three of us had done together. Because of his own relationship with Allen, he'd said that it didn't matter to him how long Allen and my pictures remained up.

Jasper had left as the sun started to set. He had work the next morning and a lot of things to do before he moved in the following Saturday. Neither one of us had wanted to wait until he could find a buyer for the house, but the idea of leaving it empty had bothered him until he'd come up with a brilliant idea. One of the reasons Jasper had wanted to start a free clinic was to help the people in St. Helena who couldn't necessarily afford quality healthcare. One of the things he'd wanted to do eventually as well was to set up a place where families in need could stay while they were getting back on their feet. While his house wasn't big enough for multiple families, it could be enough for one.

I'd been so excited when Mitchell had pulled in that, for a moment, I'd forgotten the way my brother had left that morning. I'd practically thrown myself into Mitchell's arms, declaring that I'd had wonderful news.

The moment I'd said the words, however, I wished I could've taken them back. My brother's face had darkened and he'd given me one of his scowls. The conversation had been brief but harsh.

"What do you mean you asked Jasper to move in with you?" Mitchell's voice was sharp.

"I care about him, Mitchell, and we enjoy being together. I have this huge place but I'm all alone here—"

"I'm here."

"I know you are." I tried to placate him. "And I really appreciate you staying with me, but you have your own place."

"So does he."

I took a deep breath and tried to speak calmly instead of slapping my idiot brother like I desperately wanted to. "Jasper and I want to be together and this was the step we wanted to take. Together."

"What about Allen?"

"I loved Allen," I said. My heart constricted, but it was more of a wistful pain than agonizing grief. "But he's gone. And I know he would've wanted me to be happy."

"With his best friend?" Mitchell snorted a laugh. "Come on, Shae. You can't be serious. Allen was your husband. You were with him for eight years and now, four months after he dies, you're shacking up with his best friend?"

"Just because my husband died doesn't mean I have to stop living," I said, stung. I'd expected some resistance, but not this.

*"Mom never dated after Dad died. She loved him until the day she died."*

I nearly flinched. *"That's not fair and you know it. I'm not her, Mitchell."*

*"That's obvious,"* he snapped.

*"If you don't like it, you don't have to be here."* I put my hands on my hips. *"Go home."*

*"Gladly."* He started to stomp off towards the guest room where he'd been staying, but he couldn't resist landing one final blow before he went. *"I'm just glad Mom's not here to see this. She would've been ashamed of you."*

That comment had hit me hard. I'd spent the rest of the night alternating between crying and raging. Only after I'd spent hours curled up in bed, desperate for sleep, did I remind myself that it was my life, not my brother's or my mother's, that Jasper and I knew that Allen would want us to take care of each other. That he'd want us to be happy. As long as we knew that and we cared about each other, it didn't matter what anyone else said.

I'd spent the rest of the week focusing on Jasper moving in and ignoring the fact that Mitchell never called or texted. Monday after school, I'd gone through the living room and packed up some things to make room for some of Jasper's things. The kitchen had come next, though he'd decided to leave most of his own kitchenware for whatever family took up residence. The same would be done with most of his furniture, so there wasn't really much of mine and Allen's things I had to pack away.

I'd left off the bathroom until Wednesday,

throwing away the last of Allen's belongings there. I hadn't been consciously keeping around things like his razor or his brand of mouthwash, but I hadn't thrown them out either. That night, I had. I'd cleaned out every last bit of Allen from the master bathroom and then I'd sat in the shower and cried until the water turned cold.

Thursday had been even worse. I'd packed up all of Allen's usable clothes and thrown away the ones that couldn't be donated. For some reason, taking out the trash had bothered me more than putting the boxes of clothes into my car. Even though it had been late, I'd driven into the city and dropped the things off at the mission, hoping I'd be able to keep from crying.

I had. I'd actually felt good as I'd driven away, as if the thought of Allen being able to help someone even after his death had been somehow helping me heal. And then I'd seen the trashcans at the end of the driveway and I'd known that the bags inside had contained all of the little junk that Allen was never going to use again.

It had been that, more than anything else, that had made it hit home. Allen was gone and never coming back. He'd never use up the rest of the aftershave I'd bought him for Christmas last year. Never throw out the cheap comb that he'd always insisted worked 'just fine' even though he'd just as often borrowed my hairbrush.

Yesterday hadn't been any easier, coming home and feeling the house half-empty. It hadn't really looked much different. Even the upstairs had been the same until I'd opened the dresser or closet. I'd doubted that anyone else would've even noticed, but I had. I'd felt like something had been torn out of me or away from me, like a part of me had gone missing.

I'd cried myself to sleep and had woken up this morning with a new resolution.

I was moving forward. I wouldn't forget Allen or the years we'd spent together, but I wasn't going to let them hold me back either. I got up, put on a pair of ratty jeans, an equally grubby t-shirt and then headed downstairs to make myself some breakfast.

Jasper arrived a couple hours later and immediately pulled me into his arms for a thorough and resounding kiss. I melted against him, letting myself enjoy the solid feel of his body, the heat of his skin.

When he finally broke the kiss, we were both breathing hard and I was feeling much better.

Jasper frowned as he looked around. "Did Mitchell have to work today?"

I looked away. I hadn't told him about the fight. "No, he went home. After all," I tried to keep my tone light, "it'd be a bit awkward to have my big brother here too."

"Well, I didn't think he'd be staying, but I figured he'd at least want to make sure everything was set before he left." Jasper took a step back. "When did he leave?" When I didn't answer, he spoke again, "Shae, what's going on?"

"He's mad about you moving in," I blurted out. Jasper was the one person I could be completely honest with. I didn't want to start things off with a

86

lie, even a little one.

I glanced up and saw that his face had darkened.

"What did he say?"

I shook my head and reached down to take his hand. "It doesn't matter."

"It does to me." He tucked a wayward strand of hair behind my ear.

I sighed. "Short version? He thinks I'm a horrible person for even considering wanting to be with someone after Allen."

"He doesn't think that," Jasper argued. "Your brother loves you. He couldn't think anything bad about you."

The muscle in my jaw twitched. "He said my mother would be ashamed of me."

Jasper swore as he pulled me into his arms again. He kissed the top of my head as his fingers made soothing motions on my back.

"Your brother's being an asshole," he said. "Everything you've said about your mother tells me that she'd want you to be happy."

"I think she would've liked you," I said, pressing my face more firmly against his chest. Damn, he smelled good.

"I hope so."

Jasper sounded sad. I pulled back just enough so I could see his face.

"Are you okay?" I asked. I hoped I hadn't been so caught up in my own drama that I'd missed something important.

"I never wanted to come between you and your brother," he said. "Maybe I should just go home."

87

"You are home," I said firmly. "Unless..." My heart sank. "Unless you don't want to move in. It's okay if you don't. You didn't have to agree..."

He pressed his lips against mine to silence me. It was short, but firm. "I want to live with you," he said, keeping his mouth close enough to mine for me to feel the heat of his breath. "You have no idea how much I want this." He rested his forehead against mine. "To wake up next to you every morning. To know that I'm coming home to you every night. It means everything to me."

"But?" I prompted.

"But I can't make you choose between your family and me."

"Jas." I put my finger on his lips, stopping him before he could say anything else. "You aren't making me choose. Mitchell is. And if he really loved me, he wouldn't do that." I smiled. "Besides, I thought I made it clear that I've already chosen. I chose you."

His eyes closed as I put my hand on his cheek. His skin was smooth. He'd shaved this morning. My stomach tightened at the realization that I'd get to watch him shave in the mornings. That I'd be able to see him standing in the bathroom in front of the mirror, towel around his waist, chest bare...

Damn. I was never going to want to leave the house now.

# Chapter 11

Prior to Allen's death, I'd never actually lived alone. I'd gone from home to college where I'd had a roommate. From college to living with Allen. The longest I'd ever been alone in the house had been for a weekend once when Allen had gone on a trip to see his parents and I'd begged off, citing too many papers to grade. Even for someone who'd been used to living with other people, when I'd first moved in, it had taken me a while to get my bearings and for both of us to learn how to move around each other.

Not this time. It was strange how easily Jasper and I slipped into living together. I'd fully expected things to be awkward, at least for the first month or so, but once we'd finished unpacking on Saturday, it had felt natural to follow a normal routine. Dinner, shower, bed. Waking up next to him on Sunday hadn't been weird at all. And then last night, instead of worrying about how late he was going to stay since we had to work the next day, we just did the same thing we'd done the night before.

I wasn't sure if it was because he'd stayed here a couple of times or that we were just already so familiar with each other that we didn't have to learn each other's moods, but it was nice not to have to worry about any of that. This was different than meeting some random person and asking them to move in after only a few dates. I'd known Jasper as long as I'd known Allen, and the three of us had always been together that first year. It hadn't been until after they'd graduated that we'd had less time together as a trio.

I hadn't told anyone but Mitchell about Jasper moving in, but when Gina Edgars came by to pick me up so the two of us could carpool to work, I didn't try to hide kissing Jasper goodbye at the door. I knew Gina wouldn't judge. Of all the other teachers at the school where we worked, she was the only one I considered a true friend. She and her long-time girlfriend, Junie, lived across the road and the two of us often rode together to work.

"So," she said as she pulled out onto the road. "Jasper Whitehall."

I couldn't hear any disapproval, but I still didn't look at her when I answered, "We've been seeing each other for a few weeks and he moved in this weekend." I tensed, waiting for her to tell me that I'd moved way too fast, that it was inappropriate. She might not judge me, but she also wouldn't hold back her opinion of my behavior either.

"Good for you."

I turned towards her, startled at just how supportive she was.

Her light blue eyes sparkled as she smiled at me. "I saw the way he was with you after Allen died and at the funeral. It was obvious he cared about you and I'd been hoping you'd see it too. Then I heard that the two of you had been seen out together in town."

I flushed.

"You have nothing to be ashamed of or embarrassed about, Shae." She reached out a hand and gave my arm a comforting squeeze. "It's natural for you to want to be with someone again."

I looked down at my hands. "I know everyone's going to think it's too soon."

"Fuck what everyone else thinks."

I laughed, relief flooding through me. She was right. Jasper and I hadn't done anything wrong. It wasn't like we'd fallen for each other while Allen had been alive and had just been waiting for our opportunity. It had just happened.

"Can I be nosy about something?"

I glanced over at her to see a mischievous smile curving her mouth. I was immediately wary, knowing that when she got that look, anything could come out of her mouth. "Okay."

"How is he in bed?"

"Gina!" I stared at her, heat rushing to my face. When she burst out laughing, I smacked her arm. "Are you kidding me?!"

"Sorry, sweetie, I couldn't resist. That kiss goodbye? Damn. You could've started a fire with that kind of heat."

I was fairly sure my face must've been glowing by now.

"Seriously, though." Her voice sobered. "I've always thought Jasper's had to put up with too much shit around here. He'd been a wild kid, sure, but he's a good man." She reached over and took my hand. "You two deserve to be happy."

"Thank you." I swallowed hard around the lump in my throat. After Mitchell's negative reaction, I'd been bracing myself for similar responses. Having Gina's support meant a lot to me.

It took me a few minutes to regain my composure, but when I did, I couldn't resist trying to lighten the mood before we got to the school.

"By the way, the answer to your question is: amazing."

Gina gave me a puzzled look.

"How Jasper is in bed." I grinned. "I could barely walk last Monday."

Gina laughed and shook her head. "I'll make sure I tell Junie that we don't have to worry about you sitting all alone in that big house with nothing to do."

I laughed with her. "No, I'm quite sure he'll keep me busy."

As we continued to joke and tease, I let myself relax and enjoy the moment. While I was determined to move forward, I knew that there were still plenty of things that could make my life difficult in the days and weeks to come. When times like this came along, I was going to do my best to savor them.

The day went well, with all of my students behaving surprisingly well. It was still nice enough to go outside for recess and at the end of the day, since we had a little extra time, I took them out again. The smell of autumn was in the air and the sun was just warm enough. It was an absolutely beautiful day, the kind that made everything else seem brighter just because of it.

And still, I felt restless, eager to get home even though I knew Jasper was at work. I wanted to be there, with him. I loved my job and my students, but if I'd had a choice, I would've been curled up on the couch with Jasper, talking about the mundane things we'd done or had to do. I missed him the way I'd missed Allen when we'd been apart the years I'd been in college and he'd been up here.

The realization frightened me, but I didn't want it to be any other way. I wanted to want to be with him. I didn't want to be one of those people who dreaded going home, who would rather work late hours than spend time with their significant other.

By the time the end of the school day arrived, I was antsy, almost wishing I would've driven so I could leave as soon as the kids did. I knew it was a good thing, though, that I'd come with Gina and had to wait until she'd finished putting away all of her art supplies and cleaned up the bits of mess the students had missed. Jasper would be at work for another hour and a half so all I'd be doing is trading pacing here to pacing at home. At least here, my pacing also including straightening random things until my entire classroom looked as neat as it had the very first day of school.

On the drive home, Gina kept the conversation going with questions about what had been happening for the past two weeks since we'd barely seen each other. Some of her questions were about

Jasper and me, but others prompted me to tell her about the mysterious letters and phone calls, as well as Aime and Jenny. Gina wholeheartedly agreed with Jasper that Allen would've told me about a daughter if he'd known and she was even skeptical that Jenny was even his. I agreed, but I couldn't get rid of the sinking feeling in the pit of my stomach that Aime wasn't going to just go away.

When I got home, I changed out of my work clothes and into a comfortable pair of jeans and a worn flannel shirt. The best thing about my relationship with Jasper having developed the way it did was that I never really had to worry about him seeing me dressed down. He'd already seen me sick, sun-burned, grieving, and dressed in everything from my wedding dress to pajamas. I could wear what I wanted and know that he'd most likely seen me in it before.

I finished grading papers in less than an hour and then headed into the kitchen to start something for dinner. I'd gone out last week to pick up a few things that I knew Jasper liked and I was thinking about making lamp chops when someone knocked on the door. I quickly wiped off my hands and headed out, wondering if it was Mitchell coming back to apologize.

It wasn't. Instead, it was a middle-aged, weaselly-looking man with a sparse mustache and even sparser hair.

"Shae Lockwood?"

I nodded, keeping my foot braced on the back of the door in case I had to slam it shut. He didn't look

94

dangerous, but if he'd been the guy who'd started the fire and he was here to do more damage, he wasn't going to get inside without a fight.

He held out two envelopes. When I took them, he gave me a slight nod. "You've been served."

My jaw dropped as I watched him leave without any additional explanation. Served? As in legal papers?

My first thought was the Lockwoods, but when I tore open the more official-looking envelope, I saw that wasn't the case.

Aime Vargas was suing me in place of Allen for back child support and a portion of his estate.

I went back into the house and sat down on the couch. This couldn't be happening. I held up the other envelope. It didn't have anything written on it at all. I didn't want to open it, but I knew I had to know what was inside.

It wasn't another legal notice. It was a letter. From Aime.

*Shae, I know you and Jasper killed Allen so you could get his money and be together. You've deprived my daughter of her father and you owe me for that. You owe me for the years that you had with Allen that should have been mine. You're not going to fight this lawsuit. In fact, you're going to sign a statement saying that Allen is Jenny's father and you're going to give her half of everything Allen left you. You're also going to sign a statement saying that you feel so bad for taking Allen away from Jenny that you're going to pay a thousand dollars a month in child support until Jenny turns*

95

*twenty-one. If you don't do what I say, I'm going to follow through with my lawsuit and take everything. Then I'm going to call the police and tell them that Allen told me before he died that he suspected you and Jasper were having an affair. And that he was so worried the two of you might do something to him that he asked me to come forward if he died suddenly. I expect to hear from you before the court date.*

I read the letter twice, trying to figure out if she honestly thought Jasper and I had done something to Allen or if she was just using that as an excuse to blackmail me. I knew Allen hadn't talked to her. The police had gone over his calls and texts to see if there had been any suspicious activity in the months before he'd died. I was pretty sure the detectives running the case would've only been too happy to tell me that my husband had been communicating with his ex-girlfriend. Even though that part was a lie, it didn't mean she didn't think I'd done something.

I didn't care about the money. If Jenny was Allen's daughter, I had no problem putting money in a trust for her – one that her mother wouldn't be able to get her hands on. But I still didn't believe that Jenny was Allen's. Not really. Part of me thought it was true just because of the timing, but my gut said that there was something I was missing.

I looked at the notice again and then at the letter, pushing aside the emotions involved so that I could only see the facts.

A few minutes later, it hit me.

A paternity test. Aime didn't want to actually go through with the court case because she knew any half-decent lawyer would be demanding a paternity test first thing. She'd written the letter to try to get me to give her the money and acknowledge paternity outside of the court without any medical proof that Jenny was Allen's child.

I needed to call my attorney. Savill Henley had helped me through all of the legal stuff that had come up with Allen's estate. He hadn't mentioned anything about Allen putting aside money for a daughter and he'd know the best way to handle the situation. The first thing he'd do, I knew, would be to get a judge to order a paternity test.

I needed Allen's DNA.

# Chapter 12

I'd thrown away too much. Allen's hairbrush, toothbrush, razor...I'd gotten rid of all of his clothes – not that I thought they'd be able to get much off of those. I couldn't find a single thing that would have enough DNA to test against Jenny's.

But that wasn't the reason I was sitting on the floor in the guest room directly across from my bedroom, crying. Again. No, that had come about because I came in here, hoping that I'd missed something when I'd cleaned things out last week, and I'd indeed found something I'd missed.

Color swatches.

It was stupid, but as soon as I'd seen them, I'd started bawling like a baby.

A baby.

This had been the guest room that Allen and I had always intended to convert into a nursery. Being the planner that he was, Allen had picked up paint swatches nearly a year ago and we'd spent more than one night in this room, sitting on the floor and holding up different colors, trying to decide which one we liked the most. We'd argued over whether or not we'd want to know the baby's sex, if we planned on painting a neutral color to keep the room as a nursery for other kids and have the older ones move out to another room. We'd talked in hypotheticals, of course, because we'd decided that we wanted to make sure we were financially and emotionally ready to have kids, but there had been no doubt in either of our minds that this would be our nursery.

I'd already cried over the children I'd never have with Allen, but when I was here, looking for some way to prove that he didn't already have a child, it hit me harder than it had before. Even if Jenny was Allen's, he'd never know. He'd never get the chance to be the wonderful father I knew he could've been. And, no matter how I felt about Aime, I also cried for Jenny. If Allen was her father, she'd never have the chance to know him, to know what a wonderful man he'd been. There would be no father-daughter dances for them. No opportunity for him to intimidate her first boyfriend or take prom pictures. No half-brothers or sisters for her to know. He'd never walk her down the aisle at her wedding.

He and I would never paint this room and fill it with all of the things that first-time parents thought they needed. We'd never argue about who was being too strict or too lenient. No family vacations. High school graduations. College. No watching our children fall in love. Get married. No excitement over grandchildren.

That stupid, cruel disease had taken all of that away from all of us and I felt every lost moment over again, as sharp and fresh as I'd felt it the day I realized I wasn't pregnant.

I was crying hard enough that I didn't hear Jasper come in downstairs or even if he called my name. All I knew was that one minute, I was alone and the next, his arms were around me and I was burying my face against his chest as I struggled to breath. I hated that I was still crying months later, but I wasn't some fictional woman who could just get over things during a commercial break.

That didn't make me feel any better about sobbing on Jasper's shirt.

He made soothing noises and stroked my back, never once asking what was wrong. He pressed his lips to my head, murmuring words of comfort as he rocked me back and forth. We sat for what could've been hours or minutes, me curled on his lap, him holding me until the tears finally subsided.

"I'm sorry," I finally said.

"For what?" Jasper pushed my hair back from my face as I looked up at him.

"For crying like this."

"It's okay," he said.

"No." I shook my head. "It's not. You moved in and I want to be with you, but I came in here and started crying about Allen and kids and..."

"Hey." He stopped my words with a gentle kiss. "It's okay. Sometimes things catch me off-guard too. I'll see or do something and think about how I wish I could tell Allen." His smile was sad. "I sometimes think about how much I'd love to tell him about how amazing you are and all of the things we do together. About how excited I am to be living with you."

"I don't regret asking you to move in," I said, needing him to know that wasn't the problem. "Or us being together, but I can't help feeling guilty. There was so much Allen and I had planned to do together. I sometimes feel like I should spend the rest of my life mourning every step we didn't get to take together."

Jasper kissed my forehead and his arms tightened around me. "You and I both know that Allen wouldn't have wanted that. He would want you to be happy. To keep living. To do things." He cupped the side of my face, his thumb running along my bottom lip. "He'd want you to fall in love again. To have a family."

My stomach tightened.

"I love you, Shae."

My head snapped up to look at him.

"You don't have to say it back. It's okay." His eyes were clear, open. "I just need you to know that I love you and, one day, I want us to look at the future together, to see the family we can have." He traced his fingers along my cheekbone and down my jaw. "I'm not saying this because I expect anything from you. I'm okay with being in the here and now with you. Just know that, when you're ready, there is a future for you that isn't dark and bleak. A future with me."

I swallowed hard. I wished I could say it back to him. Tell him that I loved him. But I couldn't. Not yet. I cared about him as more than a friend, but I couldn't say the word. I could, however, show him how much he meant to me.

I wrapped my hand around the back of his neck and pulled him down for a kiss. Fierce, hot and wet, I put everything I was feeling into the way my lips moved with his, how my tongue explored his mouth, how my teeth scraped and nipped his lips. Everything I couldn't say, I poured into my body.

I felt his surprise for a moment and then he was kissing me back, his hand sliding up my side to cup my breast through my shirt. I arched my back, needing him to touch me more. His hand tightened as he flipped us over, his body pressing mine to the floor. My legs wrapped around his waist and I ground against him.

"Shit," Jasper growled. His eyes were squeezed shut and I could feel the tension radiating off of him.

I started to chuckle, but the sound was lost in a gasp as Jasper pulled open my shirt, sending buttons flying everywhere. I barely had time to care about the shirt because his mouth was on me, sucking and licking and biting every inch of my skin until I was writhing beneath him.

I dug my fingers into his hair, moaning as he worked one hand between us, undoing the button on my jeans with an ease that surprised me.

"Jas," I gasped his name as he shoved his hand further into my jeans, shoving aside my panties even as I spread my legs to let him touch me right where I needed him. I swore as he slid his finger inside me.

"Come for me, baby." He pressed the heel of his hand against my clit and a shudder ran through me. "I want you to come on my hand." He ran his teeth over my ribs as his hand continued to work between my legs.

"I want you inside me." I grabbed the shoulders of his shirt.

"Later." He licked a path from my bellybutton, up between my breasts. "Come first." He pulled down the front of my bra, making an appreciative sound as my breasts came free.

I squirmed, moaning as his tongue began to circle my nipple. How did he know how to do such wonderful things with his mouth? Who had taught him?

I pushed the thought aside. I didn't want to know.

I'd seen his girlfriends, at least the ones who'd warranted introductions. I didn't know how many other women there had been. If I had anything to say about it, there wouldn't be any more.

He twisted his fingers, driving thoughts of Jasper's previous women from my mind. Pleasure coursed through me. I pushed against his hand, desperate for release. Desperate for the oblivion that came with it, however brief.

My body tensed, arched, and as his hand rubbed against me, I came. I shook beneath him and his lips moved against my skin. Words I could feel but not hear, but feeling them was enough.

While I was limp, pliant, Jasper pulled off my clothes, stopping every few seconds to kiss a new spot. I watched him with hooded eyes as he caressed and worshipped my body. I'd never seen anyone look at me the way he did.

He loved me.

I'd already known it, I realized. Before he'd said it. I'd seen it on his face, in his eyes. I'd felt it in his touch, when he'd held me, soothed me, cared for me. No matter how impulsive or rough the sex had been between us, for him, he'd always been making love.

He shifted so that he was on his knees and pulled his shirt over his head. My stomach clenched as he started on his pants. He was so beautiful, his body hard and muscled. He was so different than Allen had been, and it surprised me how I could feel so strongly about two men who were polar opposites.

"You're doing it again." Jasper smiled down at me.

"Doing what?"

"Every once in a while, you seem to go somewhere else." He stretched out next to me. He ran his fingers over my stomach and then down to just above the thin layer of curls between my legs. "I saw it before, when my fingers were inside you. For a few seconds, you weren't here." He hesitated, his eyes following the movements of his hands. "Were you thinking about Allen?" His gaze flicked up, then away. "It's okay if you were. I mean, I'd understand. You were with him for eight years..."

"I wasn't thinking about Allen." I put my hand over his, bringing it up to my mouth.

Jasper's breath caught as I took his fingers into my mouth. I ran my tongue around and over his skin, tasting myself as I cleaned his fingers. When I looked up, his gaze was heated, but I could still see the concern on his face. This time, however, I knew the concern was only partially for me. He wanted to make sure I was okay, but I could also see the insecurity there. He'd been so understanding of all the times I'd mourned Allen, never once making me feel like I should focus on him. He deserved to know the truth, even if it embarrassed me.

"I wasn't thinking about Allen," I said again as I put his hand on my breast.

"Then what?" he asked, rubbing his thumb across my nipple. Little ripples of electricity coursed across my skin. "Or who?"

"You," I said. I traced his lips with my finger as heat rose to my cheeks. "I was actually wondering who taught you all that."

"All that?" He made a face like he didn't understand.

"Dammit. You're going to make me say it, aren't you?" I shook my head. "What you do," I said. "With your fingers. With your mouth. I was wondering who taught you how to do that."

He tilted his head as he caught my hand, pressed his lips against my palm. "You're telling me that you were thinking about the women in my past?"

When I nodded, he chuckled, that same low sound that always made things deep in my stomach flip and twist.

"Glad I could amuse you," I said wryly.

He leaned over me, giving me a slow and thorough kiss, rekindling the flame that had faded to a smolder as we'd talked. His fingers teased and played with my nipple as his tongue twisted inside my mouth, not stopping until I was panting.

"Do you really want to know?" he asked, kissing my cheek and then my jaw.

"Know?" I could barely remember what we were talking about.

"About the women I've slept with before." The hand on my breast slid down my stomach. "I'll tell you what you want to know, but I'd rather be inside you, making you come again."

I wrapped my arm around his neck and pulled him on top of me. "I like that better."

His mouth covered mine as I wrapped my legs around his waist. I moaned as he slid inside me with one long, slow movement. He rested his forehead on mine as he stilled for a moment, letting both of our bodies adjust to being together. I rocked against him, reveling in the feel of him inside me, filling me.

He didn't say anything as he began to move, his thrusts deep and unhurried. The carpet was rough against my back, my ass, but I didn't care. All I cared about was the hot pleasure that every stroke sent through me, the desire in his eyes as he looked at me.

"Stay with me," he whispered. "Stay with me this time."

I nodded. "I'm staying."

"Just us," he said. "No one else. Please." There was a note of longing in the last word.

I reached up and put my hand on his face. "I'm here, Jas. It's just me and you."

His eyes darkened and my heart twisted. How many times had we been together and he'd worried that I'd been thinking of Allen? Had he wondered, every time my eyes closed, that I was thinking of someone else?

"I can't say I love you," I said.

"I know. It's—"

"But I care about you, Jasper." I kissed his chin. "I want you. And you're the only one I'm thinking about."

"That's more than enough." He surged forward and I gasped as he hit a spot deep inside me.

Our bodies moved together, with each other, against each other. I lost all sense of time. It was as if we'd been like this forever, our bodies joined as intimately as two people could be joined. We were in our own world and nothing else mattered. Only him and me and what we were to each other.

When I came, it wasn't the explosive climax I'd experienced before, but something quieter, and yet somehow more intense. And when he followed just moments later, the sensation of him emptying into me sent another wave of pleasure through me. I held him to me, running my fingers through his hair and telling him how grateful I was that he was there.

This wasn't the life I'd pictured for myself, but I was starting to realize that it might be possible that something just as good might still exist for me. Something that I never would have imagined before. With someone I'd never expected.

# Chapter 13

I didn't look for Allen's things the rest of that night. After Jasper and I finally managed to get up, we showered and ate, then spent the rest of the night just holding each other on the couch. The next morning, he told me to wait until he came home and we'd start looking for something of Allen's together. I didn't think there was much point of searching anymore, but I agreed. The court date wasn't until the beginning of December so we had more than a month before a judge would hear it, but we needed to find DNA for a paternity test or things were going to get complicated.

By the middle of the week, I was forced to admit that complicated was going to be my new life.

There was nothing. Nothing of Allen's left in the house aside from a couple books and other things we'd shared. While getting a fingerprint from a lot of those things would've been possible, none of them had what I needed.

Finally, at dinner Thursday night, I said what I'd been thinking all day.

"I have to go talk to the Lockwoods."

Jasper swore under his breath and set down the beer he'd been drinking. "There has to be another option."

I sighed and took another drink of my own beer. I rarely indulged during the week, but this hadn't exactly been a normal week.

"I can't think of anything. Can you?"

Jasper scowled. "No. Dammit."

"I already talked to Sanders and booked a flight to Texas. I leave first thing in the morning. I figure if I just show up, they'll be more likely to at least listen."

Jasper raised an eyebrow. "You really think they're going to just give you something of their precious baby boy's because you flew all the way down there to see them."

I winced and he immediately looked guilty.

"I'm sorry. The Lockwoods just get to me."

"Me too." I reached across the table and covered his hand with mine, squeezing to let him know I wasn't angry. "But if I had another option..."

"I'm going with you."

The expression on his face said he was steeling himself for an argument. When I smiled, it shifted to confusion.

"I was hoping you'd say that. I booked two tickets." I let my relief show on my face. "I don't think it's a good idea for you to come to the house with me, but I don't want to be down there alone."

I could tell he wanted to argue about me going to the house by myself, but he didn't. We had a plane ride for him to do that, and there, I'd be a captive audience. Sure enough, the moment we settled in our seats, he started in, explaining all of the reasons why he should come with me. Halfway into the trip, I dragged him back into the bathroom and 'convinced' him to let me do things my way. The flight attendant on our way back gave us a knowing look as we walked the narrow aisle back to our seats, a slightly smug smile on Jasper's face.

We landed in Texas just after noon and I took a rental car straight to the Lockwood house. The longer I waited, the more anxious I'd become. Our flight home wasn't until Sunday because I didn't believe the Lockwoods would give me what I needed. I figured I'd need most of the weekend to work on them. Jasper was going to the hotel to check in and I planned to meet him there when I was done.

The drive was forty of the longest minutes of my life. I almost wished I'd let Jasper come with me. It would've been nice to have someone to hold my hand while I thought about what to say, how to approach them. How do you tell the family of your late husband that he might've fathered a child with an ex-girlfriend almost a decade ago? Especially when said family despised you and had already made it clear that they'd be looking for any possible children just to contest their dead son's will.

I felt like my life was a daytime soap. All that was missing was some amnesia and a dead twin.

I pulled up the driveway and sat there for a minute, remembering the last time I'd been here. I hadn't come very often, but there had been a couple of times where I'd decided to go rather than wait at home alone. The last time had been about six months before Allen's death. His father had gone into the hospital for tests and the whole family had gone with him. Nothing had come from the tests, but I'd spent hours listening to Allen's mother and siblings sniping about me.

The house was absolutely gorgeous, just like the vineyard, but unlike my home, this one had no warmth. I'd never felt welcome here and Allen being gone just made it worse.

I was hoping that the timing would mean I'd only need to talk to May and Gregory. While Allen's older brother and his family lived in the family home, Marcus would most likely be out working with Alice's husband and the Lockwood business partner. The kids would be in school and Celeste would probably be out doing one of her charity things. She wasn't too bad to deal with though, so if she was home, it wouldn't make too much of a difference.

I knocked on the door and, a minute later, the door was opened by an older gentleman in a full suit despite the fact that it was in the eighties. November in Texas was much warmer than it had been back home.

"I need to speak with May or Gregory." I gave him the most pleasant smile I could muster. "I'm Shae."

Based on the way the man's mouth tightened, I didn't need to explain any further who I was. He nodded briefly and stepped aside, indicating that I should come inside. He showed me to the front

112

sitting room and then left to go get May. The fact that he'd put me in there spoke volumes about how the Lockwoods viewed me. I wasn't family. I was a guest.

"Shae." May's voice was cold. "What are you doing here?"

I gave her a small smile, just as icy as hers. "You may want to sit down for this."

She scowled, but did as I suggested. Her posture was stiff and straight, lips pursed and knees primly crossed, every inch of her telling me that my presence wasn't welcome.

"Do you remember a young woman named Aime Vargas?" I began. "She dated Allen before I met him."

"Yes, I remember." May gave me a smug look. "I liked *her*."

I ignored the insult.

"She came to my house earlier this week." I tried not to let May see me twisting my fingers together. "And she had a little girl with her. Eight-and-a-half years-old, named Jenny. Aime's claiming that Allen is Jenny's father."

Predictably, May's lips curved up into a smile. "That must've been quite a shock, to know that Allen had loved someone enough to have a child with her."

A pang went through me, but I pushed it aside. "She's filing a lawsuit and wants a portion of Allen's estate." I figured the money part of it might get her attention.

Apparently, I was wrong. She cared more about hating me than she did about the money.

"She should have it. As Allen's daughter, she's entitled to far more than you are." She sneered at me. "Thank you so much for bringing her to our attention. We'll make sure we provide Jenny with the best lawyers available so she can get everything she deserves."

I could feel my temper starting to rise and again wished that Jasper was here with me, if only to help keep me calm. I could manage it myself, but it wasn't easy, especially when I was dealing with the Lockwoods.

"We don't know for sure that Jenny is even Allen's. That's why I'm here." I took a slow breath. "I need someone in the family to donate blood for a paternity test."

"We will do no such thing!" May snapped as she stood. "In fact, we will support Jenny's claim in every way we can, even if it means standing by her with no proof."

I stared at her as I stood. "You really hate me that much that you won't even bother doing a test to see if she really is Allen's daughter?"

"Don't you dare act like you care about this family." Two spots of color showed high on May's cheeks. "Not after you've been shacking up with Jasper Whitehall not four months after my son died."

Shit.

"For all I know, you and that worthless piece of trash were fooling around behind my poor boy's back."

I wanted to scream at her that I never cheated

on Allen, that my relationship with Jasper wasn't any of her business, that Jasper was a good man and Allen had known that. I wanted to tell her every nasty comment I'd swallowed over the years.

Instead, I turned and walked out without a word, ignoring her shouting after me about what an ungrateful whore I was.

# Chapter 14

I drove half a mile before finally pulling over to the side of the road and giving in to the tears. I pounded my hands on the steering wheel and screamed in frustration. How could she do this? How could she sit there and say that she would rather let some stranger claim to have had a child with Allen than take a simple blood test. If Jenny truly was Allen's, I would give her everything. I didn't care. And I felt bad for the girl either way. But I didn't want everyone to think that Allen had abandoned his daughter. I didn't understand how May could want that for her son's memory.

I yelled and cursed, let myself vent everything until I finally had enough control to trust myself driving again. I didn't bother texting or calling Jasper as I headed towards the hotel. He'd know soon enough how badly it went. Not that either of us had expected it to go well.

He took one look at my face and wrapped me in his arms without a word.

I didn't cry again. It seemed I'd used up all my tears today, but I accepted the embrace for the support it was meant to be. Once I shared with Jasper what May had said, we both needed it.

I'd booked us a fairly expensive hotel, figuring we'd appreciate the comfort after dealing with the Lockwoods. The best part about it was the massive tub that was big enough for both of us. We didn't make love or even do anything remotely sexual, just held each other as the hot water cooled around us.

It wasn't until we were wrapped in the soft cotton of the hotel robes, lying side-by-side, that I spoke again.

"What am I going to do?"

Jasper pulled me back more tightly against his chest. I had to admit, I wasn't really in the mood for sex at the moment, but I wouldn't have minded if there had been fewer clothes between us, just so I could feel his skin against mine.

"You mean what are *we* going to do," Jasper corrected.

"We?" I echoed, feeling the warmth of the word spread through my heart.

"I told you, Shae, I'm with you." He pressed his lips against my temple. "Even if it means I have to deal with the Lockwoods."

I smiled, but there wasn't any real humor in it. I put my hands on his, lacing my fingers between his.

"All right, then. What are we going to do?"

"I guess we have two choices," he said. "We can either give up and go home empty-handed, or we can try to figure out a way to get what we need."

I was silent for a few minutes, but I wasn't really considering going back without at least trying to do something. The problem was, the idea I'd had bouncing around in my head for the last couple hours was absolutely crazy.

"Allen told me once that his mother kept all sorts of things from his childhood." My fingers tightened around his. "Including his baby teeth."

"Teeth that would have his DNA." Jasper immediately knew where I was going. "We could get a subpoena for them."

I shook my head. "The Lockwoods would tie us up in court for years."

"And there's no way they'll give the teeth to us."

"That goes without saying."

He was quiet for a moment, but when he spoke again, his voice was firm. "Then we'll just have to steal them."

I didn't say anything, but I didn't have to. That was exactly what I'd been thinking we'd have to do.

---

I'd always been a level-headed person, I liked to think. The kind of person who could be counted on, who never did anything impulsive or spontaneous. Well, except for sleeping with Jasper, but it seemed like he brought out something inside me that was a little more reckless.

Case in point, I was currently sitting next to him as we parked the rental car far enough down the driveway that the house's security cameras wouldn't catch us. We were both wearing dark clothes and I had a hat to tuck my hair up in. On the console between us were a few pieces of wire, paperclips and a few other odds and ends Jasper had spent the day collecting. I'd known about his less-than-legal pastimes as a teenager, but I'd still been surprised at how easily he'd put together lock-picking tools.

We'd come to the house this morning for two reasons. One, to make one last legal attempt to get what we needed. And it was *we*, not *I*. Jasper was with me on this. It was good to feel that support again, the kind that could only come with being part of a couple.

We'd gone together to the door, not even bothering to try to hide the fact that we were together. If anything, I'd needed the strength that holding his hand gave me to face that door again. Then the door had opened and the butler had been standing there, the expression on his face even more disapproving than before.

I hadn't been sure whether or not I should've been relieved or disappointed when he'd informed us that the Lockwoods had decided to take a bit of a holiday for the rest of the weekend. They would be unreachable for the unforeseen future.

And then he'd shut the door in our faces without another word.

Whatever lingering doubts I'd had about breaking into the house vanished the moment that door closed. I'd known their absence had been intentional, a way to completely avoid me. It wasn't meant to simply be hurtful either. It had been insulting as well.

Part of me wanted to be careless about it, to trash their house, destroy things that I knew they cared about more than they did me. Which was pretty much everything, including the dust bunnies under the beds. It would be stupid and petty and childish, but the idea of imagining them coming home to all of their precious artwork torn, fine things broken, I'd have been lying if I'd said the thought of it didn't make me smile.

I wouldn't do it though. The Lockwoods would know it was me and file charges. I'd be arrested and most likely convicted. I'd lose the vineyard. I wished I could make them suffer, but I wouldn't do it at the price of my own happiness. And I meant to be happy again.

Even if I had to commit B&E to do it.

Dammit.

When we'd gone back to the hotel, while Jasper had done his thing, I'd called Henley to talk in hypotheticals about my options. He'd confirmed what I'd already suspected. We could try to force the Lockwoods to turn over anything with Allen's DNA – I hadn't been specific – but aside from the near certainty that they would bury us in legal work and try to drag things out, there was also the possibility that they'd simply say they didn't have anything. It was only my word, based on a conversation with Allen, that his mother even had kept such personal possessions.

"I can do this myself," Jasper said, reaching over to take my hand. "You can stay here. There's no

121

need—"

"Together," I reminded him, pushing aside my thoughts. "We're doing this together."

He smiled at me and leaned over to kiss my cheek. "All right. Since I get to introduce you to the world of criminal activity, follow this very important rule: don't leave my side."

I smiled. "I don't intend to."

There was a moment of heat between us, and then we were out of the car and heading for the house.

The second reason we'd gone earlier today had been to observe the property. That had actually been more Jasper's thing and it had apparently gone well. He'd noticed a small side door that was out of view of the main security cameras. Between the both of us, we'd been able to remember that it had been an old servants' entrance, one that the Lockwoods most likely still made their servants use. It would also lead to a back staircase that would prevent us from having to go around the front and risk being seen. The butler lived in a small guesthouse behind the main house, but I knew the Lockwoods had at least one live-in housekeeper or maid. They wouldn't be wandering around at night, but if they heard an odd noise, they might call the butler or the cops.

I followed Jasper around to the side door and watched as he set to work. Less than a minute passed and I heard a click. The door opened and Jasper looked over at me. I took a breath and nodded.

It was time to break the law.

# Chapter 15

The small number of times I'd visited the Lockwood house over the years had been spent wandering around and trying to avoid Allen's family while he played nice. That meant I knew the way to the second floor from the back stairs.

Jasper and I had discussed it earlier and agreed that the bedroom was the most likely place for May to have kept the baby teeth. Allen had said that his mother had a box for each of the kids where she kept mementos of items that weren't the sort of thing to display. All of the trophies and awards the kids had earned were in the library on the first floor so anyone who came over could have the chance to properly admire the wonder that was the Lockwood family.

We moved as quickly and quietly as possible, making our way up the stairs and down the hall to the bedroom. Jasper opened the door and went in first even though we knew no one was inside. He'd made it clear that I was supposed to let him take the lead on all of this. After a moment, he whispered for me to follow.

The curtains were all drawn so I turned on my flashlight and headed for the closet. The overhead light would show under the door, but the beam from my flashlight was directed enough that it shouldn't be noticed. At least that's what we were hoping for. It still didn't stop my heart from racing as I opened the closet door and stepped inside.

"Shit," I whispered. May's walk-in closet was nearly the size of my second-grade classroom. It was lined with shoes and purses and more dresses than May could've worn in a year.

"I asked her to donate some clothes to a goodwill project I was doing a couple years back." Jasper wasn't whispering, but his voice was still quiet. "She told me that if I was trying to work off my debt to society, I needed to do it on my own."

I shook my head. "I sometimes wonder where Allen got his generosity from."

"His grandmother."

I stopped mid-step and looked over at Jasper. "What?"

"May's mother. She died his sophomore year of college and I went with him to the funeral. There were hundreds of people at her funeral. She barely had any money, but every time Allen tried to help her out, she ended up giving away whatever he gave her."

"What do you mean she didn't have money?" Allen never talked about his extended family and I'd always assumed it was because they were like the rest of the Lockwoods. Complete asshats.

Jasper gave me a half-smile. "May wasn't raised rich. 'Dirt poor' was, I believe, the term Allen used. It wasn't until she married Gregory that she had any money at all."

"You'd think that'd make her more generous, not less," I said as I continued on my way to the back of the closet.

"I gave up trying to figure out the Lockwood mentality years ago," Jasper said as he followed me.

"I think it's one of those." I pointed at three identical boxes on the topmost shelf.

Jasper reached up and pulled out the third one, assuming, as I did, that they were in birth order. He handed it down to me and I knelt on the floor before taking off the top of the box. He crouched next to me as I looked inside.

On the very top was Allen's obituary. I sucked in a breath and Jasper put his hand on my shoulder.

"I can do this if you want," he offered.

I shook my head. "It was just a shock. I can do it."

I took a moment to will my hands to still inside the rubber gloves that were making my palms sweat, then I carefully began to take out the items in the box. Allen's obituary. The newspaper story about the accident. Other newspaper clippings about the vineyard. I assumed these were secondary copies since I knew there were framed ones down in the library. I was a bit surprised to see things from Allen and my wedding, but I didn't say anything. Jasper had been there, of course, but it seemed strange to call attention to it.

"It's odd," Jasper said, breaking the silence. "Sometimes it seems like he's been gone forever, like I'm going to forget what he looked like. Other times, it's like it was just yesterday I was planning his bachelor party."

"I know what you mean," I agreed. I opened the program and looked at the names inside.

Marcus, of course, had been a groomsman and so had Randall Jackson, Gregory's business partner and husband to Allen's older sister, Alice. Also in there was Mitchell who'd reluctantly agreed to be in the wedding party. May and Gregory hadn't been happy about that, but they'd really pitched a fit about Jasper being the best man. Allen hadn't given in though.

Alice had been one of my bridesmaids and so had Celeste. Gina had tried to tell me that she and Junie were too old to be in a wedding party, but I'd begged them both. The Lockwoods had, of course, been properly mortified, but had held their tongues in public. One couldn't fail to be politically correct these days and complaining about a lesbian couple in the bridal party wouldn't have looked good for them. I'd ignored the under-the-breath commentary, happy just to have a few people there who I truly cared about.

"Did Allen ever tell you about the bachelor party?" Jasper asked suddenly.

"Are you kidding?" I raised my eyebrows. "No man tells his wife what he did at his bachelor party."

Jasper laughed. "Allen could've told you about his. He flat-out told me that if I hired a stripper, he'd never forgive me. So I rented a room at Allen's favorite restaurant and the five of us sat and drank until your brother decided we should all get tattoos."

"Mitchell?"

Jasper nodded. His eyes took on this faraway look. "He said he'd go first, but none of us thought he'd go through with it. He did though."

I quickly ran through images of my brother in my mind. How had I not seen a new tattoo?

Jasper grinned. "It's on his ass."

I laughed. "What did he get?"

"Pluto."

"Like the cartoon?"

"No." Jasper shook his head. "The planet."

"Why?" There didn't seem to be any other question to ask.

He shrugged. "I'm not sure. He just got it and left, said he was going to go find some woman to show his tattoo."

"What about the rest of you?" I frowned. "I know Allen didn't have a tattoo, so he must have backed out. Did you?"

"None of the rest of us got them," he said. "Marcus was supposed to go next, but the needle touched him once and he threw up all over the tattoo artist. Got us all kicked out. He was so pissed at me, said if I'd just hired a stripper, it wouldn't have happened. He and Randall left."

"What did you and Allen do then?" I asked, trying hard not to laugh out loud, remembering I was supposed to be quiet.

"We went back to my place and drank and

talked until we fell asleep. Very boring stuff."

"Did *you* want to hire a stripper?"

He grinned at me. "I wasn't the one getting married."

My eyes narrowed. "That doesn't answer my question."

"Of course I wanted a stripper." He reached out and took my hand. "I hadn't been out with anyone in months." We were silent for a moment and then he asked, "What about you?"

"What about me?" I slid my hand from his and reached back into the box to pull out Allen's college grade cards.

"Did you have a stripper at your bachelorette party?"

I laughed, then clapped a hand over my mouth as I realized how loud the sound had been. After a moment, I took my hand away and answered his question. "Of course not. Do you honestly think May Lockwood would've let that happen?"

"But Gina was your maid of honor."

I nodded. "Yes, and as she pointed out, she was the last person who should be choosing a stripper for a heterosexual bachelorette party." I set aside a clipping of the UCLA Dean's list from Allen's freshman year. "I ended up with something that looked like a cross between afternoon tea and some sort of hippie meditation ritual."

His eyebrows went up.

"Seriously." I shook my head at the memory. "I was just glad when it was all over."

Another few minutes of silence fell as I

continued to dig deeper into the box.

"Does it hurt? Thinking about your wedding?"

"Not exactly." I didn't look at Jasper as I answered. "It's sad, but not painful. Not like before." I didn't add that I knew it was because of him. That he was the reason I could think about Allen without wishing I'd died too, without feeling that gaping hole inside my chest. One glance at his face told me that I didn't need to say it because Jasper already knew.

Finally, near the bottom of the box, I saw a small manila envelope. Inside was a lock of nearly white-blond hair...and a handful of baby teeth. I stared at them, forcing back a wave of pain and took a small plastic bag from my pocket, placing two of the teeth inside it. The rest I returned to the envelope.

We had what we came for.

I quickly put everything back into the box, doing my best to have it stacked the same way it had been before. With any luck, May wouldn't even notice anything was gone.

I'd just put the lid back on the box when I heard it. A creak that seemed as loud as a thunder clap.

Someone was opening the bedroom door.

# Chapter 16

We were so screwed.

I froze, not knowing what to do next. What could we do? We were in the closet, the first place someone would look if they suspected an intruder. And that had to be it, right? What other reason would have someone opening the door to the one room we just happened to be in?

The air rushed out of my lungs as Jasper grabbed me and rolled us both under a section of floor-length evening dresses. In nearly the same motion, he kicked the box so it slid across the floor to the other side of the closet. And then I was lying underneath him, his hand across my mouth as we both waited to see what would happen next.

All in all, what Jasper had done had taken mere seconds and the noise we'd made had been minimal, but there was always the chance someone could see us. He'd clicked off our flashlights and the darkness was so complete that I couldn't even see his face even though I knew he was close enough for me to feel the heat of his breath.

"Let's see what new jewelry you have, Mrs. Lockwood."

I felt Jasper stiffen in a surprise that mirrored my own. It was a woman's voice, most likely the live-in housekeeper or maid, but it didn't sound like she was there for us. In fact, it sounded like she was doing something she'd done before.

As the two of us lay there under the dresses, we listened to the young woman talking to herself. Most of it was muttered too low for us to hear the words, but the accompanying sounds of things being moved around, combined with what we could hear, told us that she made a habit of stealing various pieces of jewelry from May and that the other woman had no idea that anything was missing.

While my heart was racing in response to the fear of being caught, I couldn't help but feel a little relief at the confirmation that May wouldn't be likely to notice that things in her closet had been disturbed. With a start, I realized that even if May did notice, it was more likely that she'd lay the blame at the feet of the person who'd been stealing her jewelry as well. I felt a small pang of guilt, then reminded myself that it wasn't like I was framing an innocent girl for stealing something expensive. I'd taken two baby teeth and nothing else. The girl was the one taking May's jewelry to begin with.

Jasper took his hand off of my mouth and I felt his fingers tracing over my jaw and cheek. The gloves he wore felt strange against my skin, but the gesture was as comforting as he'd meant it to be. I shifted underneath him, unable to stop a smile when

I heard him stifle a groan. His body was stretched out on top of mine and I could feel every breath he took...and that he was starting to get hard.

I knew it was in response to the situation, the adrenaline racing through our veins, but still, arousal flared hot and bright inside me. I pushed my hips up against him and heard him suck in a breath. Even though I couldn't see him, I knew he was glaring at me. I reached up into the dark and wrapped my hand around the back of his neck. As I pulled his head down, I wished that I could feel the heat of his skin, the way his hair felt against my fingers, but I knew better than to take off the gloves. What I was doing was risky enough.

I could feel the brief and furious argument he had with himself when our lips met, but as soon as I pushed my tongue into his mouth, I knew I'd won. His body shifted from protecting me to covering me and he kissed me back. We could still hear the maid moving around in the bedroom, but she didn't seem to matter that much. All that mattered was the firm pressure of his cock against my leg and the way his mouth moved against mine.

The instant we heard the bedroom door close, Jasper rolled us out from under the dresses, his kisses rougher as he licked and bit my lips. I writhed beneath him, wanting him, needing him. I didn't care where we were or that it was dangerous. I just needed him.

I somehow managed to shove down the front of his pants and wrap my hand around his cock. He tore his mouth away from mine and swore. I still couldn't see more than the faintest of outlines, but I knew how he would look, the way his eyes would be glittering, a dark, stormy gray.

"Shae." My name was little more than a growled whisper.

"Now." I squeezed him and he swore again.

I felt him hesitate and leaned up to nip at his throat. Suddenly, he was turning me over, his hands tugging down my pants and underwear all at once. Heat rushed through me and my nipples hardened. One hand pulled on my hips, raising my ass slightly and then he was there, nudging between my legs. My pants were around my calves, barely letting me spread my legs, but it was enough.

I shoved my forearm into my mouth to stifle my cry as he shoved inside me. I was wet, but there had been no foreplay, no stretching, and I was almost too tight. I squeezed my eyes shut, focusing on breathing as he rocked against me. There was none of his previous gentleness, no waiting to see if I was all right. He thrust into me, hard and fast, not a pause between strokes. Each one went deep and stretched me wide, filling me completely. Pain and pleasure twisted together, deep in my belly, then spread out like some hot, molten liquid coating my insides. Everything inside me was tight, waiting for the rush of release.

And then his hand slid under me, his fingers bare as they pressed against my clit. I nearly screamed as he started to rub, his touch as rough as the rest of what he was doing. I clawed at the carpet as his fingers made harsh circles over my clit, moving in perfect sync with every snap of his hips. I felt his rhythm falter and knew he was close. Then his thumb was pressing against my asshole, the pressure foreign enough to make me squirm, but he was too strong and the tip of his thumb pushed past the ring, sending a new sort of burning through me. I gasped, the muscles in my arms and legs quivering from the sensation overload. He pulled my hips higher, forcing my face against the carpet, and his fingers pushed hard against my clit.

I came so suddenly that all the air rushed out of me, leaving my mouth open wide in a silent scream. Spots danced in front of my eyes and my body tried to curl in on itself, but Jasper held me still, driving deep inside me once, twice more. On the third thrust, he made a small sound and I felt him coming, his cock pulsing inside me. His hands tightened, making my eyes roll back as his fingers pressed painfully against my over-sensitized clit. His other fingers dug into my ass until I knew it was going to bruise.

My body was still shaking even as he finally pulled out and rolled off to the side. It took me a couple minutes to recover enough to roll over and pull up my pants. I grimaced at the feel of his cum soaking my panties, but we didn't have time to clean up. We had to go.

Jasper was up already and a beam of light cut through the darkness. Without a word, he found the box and put it back where it belonged. Then he turned to me and held out his hand. His gloves were both back on. I took the slick grip and let him help me to my feet. In silence, we made our way back down the stairs, through the door and down the driveway to the car.

I winced as I sat down and saw a shadow cross Jasper's face. He didn't say anything until we were halfway back to the hotel.

"I'm sorry." He didn't look at me as he apologized.

"For what this time?" I asked with a sigh.

"I should've known better," he snapped. "It was dangerous and stupid."

"I was the one who was all over you. I instigated it."

He gripped the steering wheel so tight that his knuckles turned white. "I hurt you."

I frowned at him, puzzled. "What are you talking about?"

"Come on, Shae, I'm not stupid. I saw how you were walking, how you sat down. Shit, you have rug burn on your cheek."

Well, that explained why my cheek was stinging.

"This isn't the first time I've been sore after sex with you," I reminded him.

The expression on his face said it all.

"You didn't realize it before?" I asked, surprised. "That weekend after our date at Tra Vigne, every time I moved I felt it."

He pulled over to the side of the road and turned towards me, pain in his eyes. "Why didn't you tell me? I asked you if I was too rough and you said you were okay, that you liked 'variety'."

"And I was telling the truth. I was great." I tried

to lighten the mood. "Just made work a bit more interesting the next day."

"Shae, baby." He took my hands and raised them to his mouth, kissing my knuckles. "I never meant to..." His head dropped. "I should move out."

"What? Where the hell is that coming from?" I yanked my hands away from his.

He raised his head, but still didn't look at me. "Allen."

"I don't understand." That was an understatement. I had no clue what was going on in Jasper's head, only that I definitely didn't like it.

"When we were in there and looking at all that stuff, talking about your wedding, it was...I don't know. It just reminded me how much I'm not like Allen. And then you kissed me and I was angry."

"Angry?" I felt like a bucket of ice water had just been dumped on me, a large chunk of it settling in my stomach.

He raked his hand through his hair. "I just wanted you so much and I didn't want you to be thinking about Allen and..."

"I wasn't thinking about Allen," I snapped. "I was thinking about you. I wanted to have sex with you. I wanted you to fuck me."

"But I was too rough!" He smacked his hand on the steering wheel. "Allen never would've done that to you." He let out a shaky breath. "I just have such a hard time controlling myself when I'm with you."

The ice inside me suddenly evaporated as his words sent heat through me. I leaned forward and put my hand on his arm.

"You're right," I said. "Allen was never like that with me. But you're not Allen."

"No fuck," he muttered.

"I don't want you because I think you're him." I curled my fingers around Jasper's chin and forced him to turn his face towards mine. "If I didn't like something, I'd tell you. And I like how you make me feel. I love it." I lightly touched his lips. "You bring out something in me that I never knew existed."

He caught my hand, his grip almost painfully tight. "I don't want to lose you."

I leaned forward until my forehead rested on his. "I'm not going anywhere, Jas."

He slid his hand up my arm and around to the back of my neck, his skin cold against mine. "I'll do better. Control myself better."

"No," I said firmly. He raised his head so our eyes met. "I liked the person I was with Allen, but I like who I am with you too, Jasper." I kissed the tip of his nose and finally got a ghost of a smile. "Besides, if you remember that weekend correctly, I scratched the hell out of your back and ass."

The smile widened, but still didn't reach his eyes. "Yes, you did." He brushed his thumb over the place where my cheek hurt. "But that's different."

"Why?"

"Because that's the kind of sex...I mean, I like taking my time too, but..." He let out a frustrated sigh. "I like a little pain with my sex. I loved feeling your nails on my skin. Feeling the sting when I showered, when my clothes rubbed against them."

"And?"

He gave me a sharp look. "And what?"

"So, you're allowed to like it when I'm rough with you, but I can't like it when you're that way with me?" I pulled back, my eyes narrowing. "Is that it? You see me as this fragile little thing who shouldn't like it when you bite her, pull her hair, fuck her hard? That's not proper, or some shit like that?" My cheeks flushed. "Well fuck you. I'm not going to sit here and justify why I'm not the girl you thought I was. If Allen's meek, breakable widow is what you want, then maybe you should move out—"

The rest of what I said was lost as Jasper grabbed me and pulled me to him, his mouth hard and demanding on mine. He yanked off the hat I'd been wearing and buried his hands in my hair, twisting and pulling it as he kissed me. My lips felt swollen by the time he released me and I couldn't speak, only gasp for air.

"I don't know how to do this, Shae," he whispered, his eyes closing as he pulled me against his chest. "I wasn't lying when I said I can't control myself around you. I've never had anyone...sometimes I feel like my body is going to explode from everything that you make me feel."

"I know what you mean," I confessed softly. "I can't say the words, Jas, but don't think for a moment that I don't feel all of that too."

"Forgive me?" he asked. "It's a lot, living up to the memory of someone like Allen."

"Forgiven." I tilted my head back so he could see my face. "And hear this. You don't have to live up to anything or anyone. Allen was Allen and you're you.

139

No comparing, no measuring. He's gone. You're here. There's no competition."

He smiled and kissed my forehead. "All right, then what do we do now?"

"Now," I said. "We go back to the hotel and enjoy that big bathtub again." I grinned at him. "For some reason, I'm really sore."

# Chapter 17

We got our money's worth out of the hotel room by the time we checked out Sunday morning, thoroughly enjoying the tub, the shower, the bed. When we got on the plane, all of my private, intimate parts were throbbing wonderfully. Jasper had taken his time with me once we'd gotten back last night, at least the first time. By the time we'd finally passed out, I'd lost track of how many times he'd made me come.

I napped on the flight too. Jasper's arm around me, my head on his shoulder. The weekend had taken a lot out of me, physically and emotionally. But Jasper was there, holding me, offering me the strength I didn't have. He made sure we got back to the vineyard. He made us something to eat and he tucked me into bed. He did everything that I needed, was everything I needed.

Monday morning, I got up earlier than usual and left Jasper sleeping until the alarm would wake him for work. I wanted to stop by the lawyer's office before school. I didn't think I'd be able to concentrate on work if I had to wait until after classes ended to take him the baby teeth. Aside from the fact that I'd feel really strange carrying around a bag with two teeth in it, I needed to have Henley begin whatever he needed to start to get this paternity business taken care of.

After I dressed, I took a moment to lean down and kiss Jasper's forehead. He looked so much younger when he slept. I hadn't known him when he was a kid, but I imagined he must've looked a lot like he did when he was asleep. I smoothed back his hair and resisted the urge to crawl back in bed and curl up in his arms again.

Instead, I headed to my car and drove in to Savill Henley's office. He'd been Allen's lawyer before and now he was taking care of things for me. He was good at what he did, but he didn't specialize in criminal or family law. Still, he'd assured me that he had colleagues he'd call for assistance with my newest problem.

"Shae." He stood as I entered the office. He'd once been an athletic, muscular man, but he'd gone to seed years ago, leaving him with a bit of a pot belly. His salt-and-pepper hair was thinning, but his light brown eyes were still just as intelligent as ever. He came around the desk and shook my hand. "Please, sit."

"I can't," I said. "I have to be at school soon." I reached into my purse and pulled out the bag. "These are Allen's. They should have enough DNA in them for a paternity test."

Henley stared at the bag and then at me.

"Where...?"

I shook my head. "Trust me. You don't want to know."

"Shae." His voice took on a warning tone.

"Don't." I held up my hand. "I don't want to put you in an even more awkward position than you are already."

"If you did something illegal to get these," he began.

"Then I'd probably want to talk to a criminal lawyer rather than you, right?" I smiled at him. "And then you couldn't take these and I'm back to where we started without any way to either prove or disprove that Jenny is Allen's."

He gave me a scrutinizing look and then nodded. "All right. I won't ask anything else so I'll honestly be able to say that I don't know where they came from."

"Great." I started to turn away.

"Shae." Henley's tone softened. "What if the girl is Allen's?"

I met his gaze. "Then I'll make sure she's taken care of."

"And the Lockwoods?"

"They're thrilled with the idea," I said dryly. "In fact, they're so happy about it, they don't even want to bother with the paternity test."

He looked surprised.

I laughed and the sound wasn't as bitter as I felt. "They'd rather see all of Allen's money and the vineyard go to the girl than me, even if she isn't Allen's. But I don't care about the money. She can have all of it if she's my late husband's child."

"You just don't want anyone saying that Allen abandoned his daughter."

I gave him a partial smile. "Got it in one."

"Don't worry, Shae." He reached out and patted my shoulder. "I'll make sure they put a rush on the test and then we'll deal with whatever comes next. We won't let them drag Allen's name through the mud. *I* won't let them do that."

"Thank you."

The lump in my throat stayed there the whole ride to the school. I appreciated Henley's help and I wanted to get all of this taken care of as soon as possible, but a part of me wished I could've just stayed in bed with Jasper, that the two of us could've called off work and been together. There, with him, I could've pretended that none of this was happening. While Allen's death would still be real – Jasper in my bed left no way around that fact – I could still pretend that the rest of it wasn't real.

I was starting to heal, but with each new crisis, it made it harder to move forward. The Lockwoods were still trying to get the trust, which meant I had to get a letter or a phone call every week or so from Henley to tell me what the newest step was. It was almost harvest time, which wasn't necessarily a crisis, but it was something more I needed to do without Allen. And now there was Aime Vargas and Jenny.

I pulled into my usual parking spot, but didn't get out of the car. I still had some time before I had to go inside. I rested my forehead on the steering wheel and closed my eyes. I'd managed to feel relaxed for a full day yesterday and now the tension was back. Every inch of my body was tight and the day hadn't even started.

How was I going to get through this?

My phone buzzed and I sighed as I pulled it out of my purse. The knot in my stomach eased a bit when I saw that it was a text from Jasper. It was short and simple, but it made me smile.

*Missed you this morning. See you tonight. Have a good day.*

Nothing spectacular or extraordinary. No flowery declarations. But I knew he meant every word of it, and that was what was important.

I tapped back out a response just as simple.

*Have a good day. I'll be thinking about you.*

If I couldn't tell him that I loved him, he at least deserved to know that I thought about him. And I did. The faint little twinges in my body that were leftover from our weekend made it impossible to not think about him. But, sometimes it was simple things in the oddest places. I'd think about him when I was teaching science class and wondering if any of the little boys and girls sitting at their desks might one day be doctors like Jasper. I'd think about him at lunch, wondering if he was eating now too. While I'd meant what I said to him that I wasn't comparing him to Allen, I couldn't help but notice that I was thinking about Jasper almost more than I had about Allen in a long time. I wasn't sure what to make of that though. I did know that I wasn't in the best state of mind to analyze it at the moment, so I put it aside and tried to focus on teaching.

By the time the final bell rang, I was ready to go home and crash on the couch. I didn't even feel like cooking dinner. A quick call to a nearby restaurant and at least that was taken care of. After picking it up, I headed straight home. A hot shower and a change into comfortable clothes made me relax a bit, but it wasn't until I saw Jasper's car pull into the driveway that I felt the tension start to fade away.

Then I saw the expression on his face, and my stomach dropped. His mouth was twisted into a scowl, his eyes stormy.

"Are you okay?" I asked as he came in.

I let out a squeak of surprise as he grabbed me, lifting me off the ground. His mouth came down on mine and I wrapped my arms around his neck. He bit down on my bottom lip, drawing a moan. I tugged on his hair and he sucked my lip into his mouth and my body instantly burned.

Holy hell, how did he do that?

My stomach clenched and he tilted his head, deepening the kiss until my world spun. We were both panting when he finally broke it.

"I needed that." His voice was rough as he sat me down.

"What happened?"

His eyes darkened even more and his hands tightened on my hips. "It's nothing."

"Jasper, talk to me." I reached up and ran my fingers down his cheek. "You can tell me anything."

He sighed and pulled me against him. "My parents aren't happy about me living here."

"Oh." I hadn't been expecting that. I'd only met Jasper's parents a couple times at special occasions. I hadn't thought they'd loved me, but I'd assumed they didn't have much of an opinion about me either way.

"They're upset because of how people are reacting. They're saying I'm embarrassing the family. Again." There was anger in his voice and I wrapped my arms around his waist.

Apparently, it was my turn to apologize. "I'm sorry."

"For what?" he asked, confusion on his face.

I looked up at him. "For making things difficult for you."

He chuckled and shook his head. "You're amazing, you know that? My parents are being assholes and you're apologizing. We're together and we did nothing wrong. They can either deal with it or not." He brushed his lips across mine.

"But you shouldn't have to put up with that," I said.

"You're right. And I know what I have to do." A determined expression came over his face. "It's time to stop talking about starting the clinic and just do it."

"Without the money from Allen's trust or the insurance?" I asked.

"I have enough to last me until the judge rules in your favor about the trust." He grinned at me. "Unless you were going to make me start paying rent."

"Well, the vineyard is paid off," I said, drawing

out the words. I slid my hands down to his firm ass and squeezed. "But making you work off room and board definitely sounds appealing."

"I'm at your service." He kissed me again, a little more firmly. "Just tell me what you want me to do."

"I'm sure I can think of a few things." I took his hand and started to lead him towards the bedroom. "Dinner can wait."

# Chapter 18

He did it.

Tuesday morning, he went into his father's practice and quit. I was a bundle of nerves at school, checking my phone every few minutes until I finally received a text.

*Did it. Going home now to work on plans. I'll make dinner.*

I breathed a small sigh of relief even though I was still anxious to hear the details. At least I knew that things hadn't gone so badly that I needed to call him on my lunch break. I wanted to, but knew that if I did, I wouldn't be able to concentrate all afternoon. I was already having a hard enough time this morning.

By the end of the day, I'd called three students by the wrong name, started to re-teach the previous day's social studies lesson and forgot that I had playground duty. When the bell rang, I was more than ready to go home. I stayed my usual twenty minutes after, rushing to get through spelling tests so I wouldn't have to worry about it tonight.

The smell of a roasting chicken greeted me as soon as I stepped inside the house and when I saw Jasper smile, the tension went out of me. I'd spent most of the drive home trying to think of ways to make him feel better about his parents being idiots. Judging by the expression on his face, he didn't need any of it.

"How'd they take it?" I asked after giving him a quick kiss hello.

"Actually, they seemed a bit relieved," he said as he followed me into the bedroom so I could change. "They even offered suggestions about what I should do now."

The words had a bit of bite to them and I glanced up as I pulled on more comfortable clothes.

"Apparently, they think it would be best for the family if I tried for a position elsewhere. I believe Seattle, Los Angeles and Chicago were all mentioned. Dad said he'd be happy to make a few calls on my behalf."

I was only half-dressed, but I didn't care. I crossed over to him and wrapped my arms around him. "I'm sorry."

His arms closed around me and he pressed his lips against the top of my head. "I'm not. They've had reason in the past to believe I'm going to screw things up. Now I get to prove them wrong."

With that driving him, Jasper spent the rest of the week working on his clinic. He'd managed to convince a local businessman to give him a good deal on renting a property closer to the poorer section of town, but he didn't have the money to hire someone to come in and do any renovations, so he did them himself.

I helped as much as I could, going to the clinic after school and helping him paint until late at night. It was exhausting, but satisfying. Some of that came from watching the place take shape, but most of it was from how proud Jasper was of what he was accomplishing.

There was only one downside to the whole thing. Georgia Overstreet.

She'd been the receptionist at the Whitehall family practice for a couple of years and I'd always gotten the distinct impression that she didn't like me. Now it wasn't merely an impression. I was sure of it. Two days after Jasper quit, she showed up at the clinic, asking for a job. Jasper had been excited about it when he came home, telling me that Georgia was happy to work for a fraction of what his father had been paying her and was even willing to work for free until finances balanced out. I knew he was convinced that she was a wonderful person for doing this, but I didn't trust her. She had ulterior motives to what she was doing, I was sure of it. She did, after all, have a thing for Jasper.

"Good evening, Georgia," I said with a smile as I walked into the clinic.

She spent her time organizing the filing systems and setting up the hand-me-down computer Jasper had gotten. The thing was almost archaic, but it worked and it was free. I'd offered Jasper the money to pay for something newer, but he refused. I knew, until the trust was released, he wasn't going to

151

accept money from me.

Part of me really wanted to give him the insurance money, but now that I knew the truth about what Allen had done, I felt even guiltier about taking it. And that wasn't even taking into consideration the fact that I could be in trouble for insurance fraud if it came out that Allen had committed suicide.

"Where's Jasper?" I asked as I set my school bag down in one of the waiting room chairs.

They weren't expensive, but they didn't look cheap either and they matched the rest of the room perfectly. Jasper had a surprisingly good eye when it came to décor. He'd painted the walls a soft gray color and hung a few inexpensive prints to keep it from looking too bare.

Georgia scowled at me, not even bothering to pretend to be nice since Jasper wasn't here. "Dr. Whitehall is painting the x-ray room."

"Thank you." I took my other bag with me as I headed into the back.

I made a quick stop in the bathroom to change into a pair of ratty jeans and a t-shirt, then went to the room at the far end of the hallway. Jasper didn't have an x-ray machine yet, but that was one of the things he was already planning to talk to donors about. With the ability to do x-rays in the clinic, he wouldn't have to refer as many patients to the hospitals. He'd be able to check for things like broken bones himself.

I stopped in the doorway for a moment, letting myself enjoy the sight in front of me. He was wearing clothes similar to mine – jeans and t-shirt – and they clung to his body in such a way that they showed off every muscle. It was funny when I thought about it, how I'd never really paid much attention to Jasper's body before, and now I couldn't stop thinking about it.

As if he'd felt me watching, he turned, a smile breaking across his face. He set down the paintbrush and crossed the room in just a few long strides, catching me up in his arms and giving me a resounding kiss.

"How was work?" he asked as he set me down. His hands stayed on my waist, keeping my body close to his.

"Fine," I said. "Adam Beardsley fell off of the jungle gym and was convinced that he'd broken every bone in his body."

A look of concerned alarm came over Jasper's face.

"He was fine," I said, grinning. "Two minutes later and he was chasing Marigold Carpenter around." I took a step back to look around the room. "What about you? It looks like you've gotten a lot done."

"I have," he said. "Georgia came back and helped me tape things off this morning."

I bit my tongue to keep from telling him what I really thought about his secretary. I'd caused him enough problems already. I'd just deal with Georgia. Besides, it wasn't like I was going to be working here.

"Did you eat lunch?" I asked.

He ducked his head, a sheepish expression on his face. "I was busy."

"Jasper," I said, exasperated. "You're a doctor. I shouldn't need to be reminding you to eat."

"Well, I'm hungry now." He took a step towards me, the glint in his eye telling me that he wasn't talking about food.

"Jasper." I gave him my best stern look, but he simply grinned at me and wrapped his arms around my waist. I pushed at his chest, but I could've been pushing at a rock wall for all the good it did me.

"It's been too long, Shae." His mouth pressed against my jaw. "I want you."

"What, last weekend wasn't enough?" I was protesting, but my body was already melting against him. I couldn't help it. His touch, the feel of his body against mine, the sound of his voice...all of it spoke to that deep, primal part of me.

"Never enough," he murmured as he nuzzled the spot under my ear. "I always want you. Every minute of every day."

I closed my eyes and a moan slipped out as his tongue flicked against my earlobe.

"I want you so much that it's hard to breathe." His lips brushed my mouth and he rested his forehead against mine. His arms tightened their hold and I could feel him hardening against my stomach.

I'd always known what the word *insatiable* meant, but I wasn't sure I'd ever truly understood it until I'd started this relationship with Jasper. And it wasn't only coming from him. My own need for him was just as strong. It was like an ache, a longing so deep inside that it was a part of who I was, and it wanted him, needed him. The thought of not having him, of him not being there was unimaginable, like trying to go without water or air.

"I feel the same way." My whisper was so soft that, for a moment, I thought he hadn't heard me.

Then he was lifting me off the ground and his lips were on mine. I wrapped my legs around his waist even as I slid my tongue along his, eager to feel the wet heat of his mouth. He had one arm under my ass, the other at my shoulders and still managed to open a door without even pausing in his plundering of my mouth.

I had a moment to register darkness, then something clicked and a dim overhead light came on. We were in a storage closet of some kind, one that was only half full of whatever supplies Jasper had already purchased. I didn't care about any of that though. I was more focused on getting that damn t-shirt off him.

He set me on a stack of boxes, pulling back long enough to yank his t-shirt over his head and then toss mine down to join it. He didn't bother taking off my bra, but rather simply pulled down the cups and let my breasts spill free. I buried my hands in his thick hair, holding his head to my chest as he took one of my nipples into his mouth. His tongue circled it, flicking against the tip before latching on tight and sucking hard enough to make me cry out.

"Shh." He chuckled as he raised his head. "You don't want Georgia hearing, do you?"

155

I could easily visualize the look of shock and hatred on her face if she walked in on us. Part of me almost wanted her to hear me, to come back and see the two of us. I wanted her to know that Jasper was mine because it didn't take a genius to know that she was jealous. I doubted Jasper had even noticed, but I had.

Then Jasper was using his teeth to worry my hardened nipple and I forgot about everything and everyone else. He reached between us, his hand pressing against the crotch of my jeans and I moaned, raising my hips to move against him.

"Could I make you come like this?" he asked, kissing his way back up my neck until his mouth was against my ear. His fingers pushed harder against my jeans and I swallowed a cry. "I'll bet I could. Make you come in your jeans just from my hand."

I rocked against him as I wrapped my arms around his neck. His hand began to move back and forth, using my jeans and underwear to create the most delicious friction. Shivers of pleasure washed over me and I squeezed my eyes closed. I was so close. I hadn't even realized I'd been wound this tight until he touched me.

"Come for me, baby. I want to watch you come like this."

My head fell back as he pressed hard against me. I bit down on my bottom lip, holding in the cries of pleasure that wanted to escape as he pushed me towards my release. He wrapped his arms around me, holding me as I came.

I slid my hand between us and he stiffened as I

cupped his cock through his jeans. He started to pull away, but I tightened my grasp until he stilled. When I began to rub him, he sucked in a breath.

"Shae."

"Hush," I said, my own voice breathless. "Turnabout's fair play."

I scraped my teeth over his nipple and he moaned. When I took the flat nub between my lips and began to suck, he swore, his hips bucking against my hand. He dug his fingers into my hair, twisting and pulling as if he wasn't sure he wanted me to stop or to keep going. A rush of pride went through me. I loved how I could make his body respond to me.

"I'm close." His voice was rough. "Please, Shae, I need you. Your mouth. Inside you."

"No," I said firmly. I lightly bit down on his nipple and he jerked. "I want you to come like this."

He groaned as I squeezed him and I felt a shudder run through his entire body. He wasn't kidding, he was close.

"Don't fight it." I pulled some skin into my mouth, sucking and biting until I left a mark. "Come for me, Jas. I want to see you come."

At my words, he swore, his body tensing. I felt his cock pulse under my hand and then the warmth of cum beneath my fingers. He grabbed my face between his hands and kissed me, fiercely and thorough, until my lungs were burning for air.

After a few minutes, I stood up, fixing my bra as I looked for my t-shirt.

"Where are you going?" he asked.

"To the bathroom," I said. I glared at him, but there was no anger behind it. "Since I don't have an extra set of panties here, I'm going to have to take mine off."

His eyes darkened and a stab of desire went through me.

"You should probably do the same," I said. "And maybe try to dry that spot on your jeans." I gave him a wicked smile. "Wouldn't want Georgia to know what happened."

"I have another change of clothes," he countered, pushing himself up straight.

"Nope." I shook my head. "If I have to go commando, then so do you."

He made a half-strangled sound.

"Maybe you'll work a bit faster so we can leave early tonight."

He reached out and wrapped his arms around my waist, pulling me back against him. "Or," he said. "I could send Georgia home, lock the doors and we could take our time painting, with plenty of breaks."

I smiled and leaned back against his bare chest. "I like that idea better."

# Chapter 19

Despite Jasper's insistence on regular breaks throughout the weekend, we managed to get quite a bit accomplished. So much so that, Sunday night we were able to leave at a reasonable time and spent most of the evening relaxing at home. There were only a few things left to do, Jasper said, before he'd be ready to open the clinic. I didn't understand most of how this was going to work, with some patients able to pay and having insurance, and then those who couldn't, but I trusted that he'd done his research and knew what he was doing.

It was fun watching him get excited about this. His entire face lit up when he talked about it. I remembered feeling that way about teaching, how excited I'd been as a student teacher, and then even more so when I'd gotten hired. I was still enjoying it, but much of that initial excitement was gone. Some of it, I knew, was normal for settling into a job. More of it, though, I knew was from everything else that had been going on.

I could still get excited about something or happy about something, but sustaining it for long periods of time was still difficult. Sooner or later, I started thinking about all of the chaos in my life and, that quickly, all of the positive would just fade away. If I hadn't had Jasper, there were some days I wasn't sure I would've gotten out of bed.

That was one of the reasons I'd enjoyed helping him with the clinic. It kept my mind off other things and focused on either the clinic itself and all the good it was going to do, or on Jasper and how amazing he was. With him, I was able to get a glimpse of what my life would be like when all of this was finally over. There were still times when I thought we were moving too fast, but when we were working together, talking with each other as easily as we always had, I could see how right it was. How we'd gone from being friends to being more. He was my rock, my strength. More importantly, we were good for each other, good together, and that's all that mattered.

He was also the only person who could keep me sane while we played the waiting game for the paternity test results.

Fortunately, we didn't have to wait as long as I'd thought.

Since pretty much all that was left to do at the clinic was organizing the medical supplies, there wasn't much I could do there. I'd enjoyed spending time with Jasper at the clinic – I flushed as I thought of all of the things Jasper and I had done there – but I'd also gotten behind in my schoolwork. I had a stack of tests to grade and lesson plans to make, so I came straight home from school yesterday and worked until nearly midnight when Jasper had finally gotten home. Today, I'd done the same thing and was currently sitting on the couch, feet tucked under me, working through penmanship papers.

My phone buzzed and I sighed, already suspecting who it was. Sure enough, it was a short message from Jasper. *Delivery just came in. Working late again. Miss you.*

I sent back a quick response telling him that I missed him too and to make sure he got something to eat, then I went back to my papers.

It was strange, how quickly I'd forgotten what it was like to be alone here late at night. It wasn't the same, of course, as it had been after Allen died, but it was still too quiet, too empty. I wanted to text Jasper and ask him to come home so I didn't have to eat dinner alone, so that I didn't spend my time wondering when he would be here. So I could fall asleep in his arms instead of waking up when he crawled into bed behind me.

I didn't though. The clinic was important and I didn't want to become one of those women who couldn't stand on her own two feet. Granted, it wasn't like I didn't have a good reason to need someone to lean on lately, but I still didn't want to be that kind of needy person.

I was fine for the next couple hours and fine as I went into the kitchen to get myself something to eat. I'd made a casserole yesterday and there was plenty left so I spooned out a plate and stuck it in the microwave. As I went to the refrigerator, the house phone rang. I considered not getting it on the off chance that it was the Lockwoods, but they hadn't called during the past week which led me to believe that they hadn't discovered what Jasper and I had done, which meant they'd have no reason to call me.

I picked it up. "Hello?"

"Mrs. Lockwood?"

"Mr. Henley." My stomach clenched and, suddenly, the smell of the casserole, which had been so appetizing, now made me want to throw up. I sat down on one of the chairs. I wasn't sure my legs could hold me, no matter what my lawyer had to say.

"I apologize for calling so late, but I got the test results and didn't think you'd want me to wait until tomorrow."

"No," I said quickly. "I'm glad you didn't."

"The DNA isn't a match."

I closed my eyes and felt the tears make hot trails down my cheeks. It was all I could do not to actually cry with relief.

"Allen isn't Jenny Vargas's father."

I hadn't really needed the explanation, but I appreciated hearing it out loud just the same. I put my hand over my mouth and took a shaky breath.

She wasn't Allen's. He hadn't had a child with another woman.

I wiped my cheeks. "Thank you." The words came out as weak as I felt.

"I'm sure this is a big relief for you," he said.

I almost laughed. No shit.

"But it's not completely solving the problem."

I opened my eyes and frowned. "What do you

mean?"

Henley sighed. "I know this is giving you peace of mind because you know that was Allen's DNA, but Miss Vargas is contesting where the sample of Allen's DNA came from. She has an attorney who's filing papers to force me to disclose the source, as well as who gave it to me."

"I thought that was covered under attorney-client privilege?" I asked.

"It is," he replied. "But as soon as I say that, they'll know it came from you."

"And they'll just assume that I had something of Allen's and handed it over."

"That would've worked," he said. "If the Lockwoods didn't already know that you didn't have anything."

Shit. "They're involved?"

"Not exactly," Henley said. "But they did contact Miss Vargas at the end of last week and told her that they wanted to meet Jenny."

Double shit.

I never should have told them about her. I should've just skipped over trying to do things the legal way and gone straight to the breaking and entering.

"They told her that they believed that Jenny was Allen's daughter and that they'd help her prove it."

The sick feeling in my stomach was back. "They're behind it," I said. "They're the ones telling her to question where the DNA came from."

"Most likely," he agreed.

"So what do we do now?" I closed my eyes again

and rubbed at my temples. "I mean, can they compel me to say where I got the...teeth?"

"Maybe," Henley said. "Like I told you before, criminal law isn't my area of expertise."

"Do you want me to get another lawyer?" I really hoped not. I trusted Savill Henley, and there weren't many people at the moment I could say that about.

"Not if you don't want one," he said, his tone firm. "I'll talk with some friends of mine, get their opinion on things. I'm going to do whatever needs to be done to make sure this goes away."

I nodded and thanked him automatically. There wasn't really anything else to say. Maybe good luck? Hope things go well? My emotions were a chaotic mess. I was lucky I could even think well enough for gratitude. I hung up the phone after he promised to call me as soon as he knew anything new, but I didn't move from where I was sitting.

Jenny wasn't Allen's.

He hadn't lied to me about that. He hadn't abandoned his daughter.

I should've been relieved.

I was relieved.

I pressed my fingers together to try to keep my hands from shaking. I needed to talk to Jasper. Tell him about the call. More than that, I needed to hear his voice.

I called his cell from the house phone, thankful that his number had already been programmed in. He didn't answer though. It went to voicemail and I left a brief message, asking him to call me back. I frowned at the phone as I hung up. He hadn't answered. That was strange.

I could've called the main clinic line. Jasper had given me the number yesterday, but I knew that Georgia would be the one who answered. I preferred to wait for Jasper to come home.

No, that was a lie. I didn't prefer to wait for Jasper. I wanted him here. Now.

I put my head on my hands and waited to fall asleep.

# Chapter 20

I was already asleep when Jasper came home, but him climbing into bed woke me as it always did. I rolled over before he'd even finished settling and pressed my face against his chest. He wrapped his arms around as I breathed in the smell of soap and him. The hair on his chest scratched against my cheek, but I didn't mind.

"Jenny isn't Allen's daughter." My words were muffled and soft, but Jasper's arms tightened around me. "Henley called."

"I'm glad to hear that." Jasper kissed the top of my head.

I nodded. "It's not over yet. Aime's not going to give up."

"Then we'll face it together," he said. "But at least we know the truth."

I nodded again and pressed myself even more closely against his bare skin. I didn't want to talk anymore. I just wanted to sleep. As if sensing this, he didn't say another word, only held me until I fell asleep again.

He was still holding me when I woke up the next

morning. I still had a few minutes before my alarm was scheduled to go off and I spent them looking at him. He'd been working so hard lately.

I brushed some of his hair back from his face, letting my fingers linger on his cheek. I needed to be there for him more, let him know that I supported what he was doing. We were partners in this. It wasn't all about him supporting me.

But I wasn't about to wake him to tell him that. He needed to sleep.

I slipped out of his embrace and turned off the alarm before it could wake him up. I made sure to shut the bathroom door all the way and moved about as quietly as possible. It was the first time in a week that I'd been up before him and I left for school hoping that he'd stay in bed for at least a bit longer.

I'd actually slept well last night and now, in the daylight, I could see the positive side of things. Jenny wasn't Allen's daughter. That was a fact now. Aime could question it, and if I had to, I'd admit what I'd done to get Allen's baby teeth, but no one would disparage Allen's name. And no matter what I went through, Jasper would be there.

Class went well that morning and I texted Jasper at lunch. We managed to have a decent conversation before he had to go and I began to feel like things were finally going to get better. That my life was going to be okay.

I was partway through reviewing the previous day's math lesson when all hell broke loose.

It started when the door to my classroom

opened. I assumed it was Principal Sanders coming in to see how I was doing. He'd done that quite a bit so far this year. Instead of him, however, a petite brunette came in, eyes narrowed and face flushed.

Shit.

"Aime." I kept my voice calm as I started to walk towards her.

The way my classroom was set up, there were at least half a dozen kids between me and her, and the look on her face told me that I didn't want anyone in her path, least of all my students. Any anger I had towards her was pushed aside. The kids mattered more than my own issues.

"If you need to speak with me, why don't we step into the hallway?" I was surprised at how pleasant my voice sounded.

"You bitch!"

The whole class gasped. I was pretty sure some of them had heard the word before, but they all knew it was something they should never say.

"Aime." I walked faster. I needed to get her out of the class and away from my kids. "Hallway, now."

"Don't you dare talk to me that way!"

I grabbed her elbow and steered her back through the door. I closed it firmly behind me and gave her a slight shove so that she was a few feet away. I didn't want her anywhere near me.

"You're a vindictive little whore!" She spat out the words. "You stole Allen from me. I'll be damned if you get his money too. I'm owed that!"

"You need to go." I crossed my arms over my chest to resist the impulse to slap her. "This is for

169

the courts and lawyers to decide."

"Like I'm going to let that happen." She stalked towards me. "I warned you, you cunt, what would happen if you didn't give me what I wanted!"

"We both know that Jenny isn't Allen's daughter..."

I didn't even see the punch coming. I would've thought she'd be more the type to slap and scratch. Instead, she threw a right hook that caught me right across the jaw. I swore as pain burst across my jaw and I stumbled backwards. The second time she swung, however, I was ready and I grabbed her wrist, twisting it up behind her back like Mitchell had taught me years ago. She cursed and struggled, but she was small enough that I was able to keep her contained until the school's security guards came running.

My school day came to an abrupt end as the security guards took Aime to the principal's office. I wanted to go back in and calm my class because I knew they had to be terrified after watching Aime. When the principal gave me a strange look, my cheek gave a throb and I remembered that she'd hit me. Yeah, it probably wouldn't be a good idea for the kids to see me like this.

"You're going to need to get that looked at," Principal Sanders said. "You're bleeding."

I automatically lifted my hand, wincing as I touched my cheek, then bringing it down to see my fingers sticky with blood. Aime must've been wearing a ring.

"I'm fine," I protested, trying to ignore the pain

in the side of my face.

"If you want to press charges against her for assault, you'll want medical records to show what she did."

As much as I hated to admit it, he was right. And I was going to press charges. It wasn't just about how this would make Aime look bad in front of the court either. I was seriously worried about Jenny. A mother swearing in front of her daughter was her own business. A mother using her daughter to try to get a pay-off was despicable. A mother with that kind of temper could be dangerous. I had no proof that Aime ever hit Jenny, but after what she'd just done, I wouldn't have put it past her. She obviously hadn't cared about behaving violently in front of students. And how the hell did she get in the front doors?

I considered calling Jasper, but as the ambulances were pulling in, I sent off a deliberately vague text instead. He had enough on his mind and it wasn't like he could do anything right now.

*Aime showed up at school. I'll tell you more when you get home.*

By the time the paramedics had finished looking at my cheek and bandaged it, I'd gotten a response.

*Stay there. I'm on my way.*

Relief went through me. I'd been prepared to deal with this alone, but it was nice to know I wouldn't have to.

"Shae!" Gina grabbed me in a hug, nearly knocking the wind out of me. "What the hell happened?"

171

I gave her the brief run-down after disentangling myself from her embrace. I watched as her eyes widened, then narrowed.

"I'm going to kick her ass."

She started to turn towards the school and I reached out, grabbing her arm. I would've found it funny if I hadn't known she was serious. Considering that before she'd become a teacher, she'd trained as a boxer, I didn't doubt she could do plenty of damage.

"She's under arrest, Gina, and I'm pressing charges. It's all taken care of."

Gina scowled, her eyes flashing. "I can't believe Allen ever dated someone like that."

"It was nearly ten years ago," I said. A part of me thought she had a point, but I didn't say that. "A lot can change in a decade."

She didn't have time to respond, however, because the school doors were opening and two officers came out with Aime between them. She didn't struggle as they escorted her to the police car, but she did give me the kind of glare that could only be described as deadly. Another officer came my way and I was relieved to see that he was a regular uniform, not either of the detectives I'd had the pleasure of speaking to before.

"Mrs. Lockwood, a word?"

I gave him a tight smile and nodded. I was really getting sick of having to give statements to the police. I kept mine as short and to the point as possible, unable to keep myself from looking over at the entrance for Jasper's car. I'd just finished telling the officer about how I'd pinned Aime's arm behind her back when I saw the car. My heart gave a thud.

"Is that all?" I asked.

The officer followed my gaze and smiled as Jasper got out of the car. "Yes, ma'am. If we need anything else, we'll call you."

I barely heard the last part as I was being enfolded in Jasper's strong arms.

"Oh, baby," Jasper murmured as he gently touched the side of my face. "We need to get some ice on that."

"I'm okay," I said. I tightened my arms around his waist and let the safety I felt with him slide over me. "And you're here, so I'm good now."

Before either of us could say anything else, my cell phone buzzed. It wasn't a text though. It was a call. I would've left it, except I was waiting for Henley's call. I managed to get my phone out without leaving Jasper's arms.

"Mr. Henley?"

"Shae, you're not going to believe this. I think I may have just found a huge break. Do you think you can go into work late tomorrow? I need you to come by the office."

I looked over at Principal Sanders who was talking to the same officer I'd given my statement to. "I think that can be arranged. What time do you want me there?"

# Chapter 21

Part of me wished that Mr. Henley had told me over the phone what he'd found, but another part was glad that I didn't have yet another thing to deal with at the moment. My cheek was throbbing, my nerves frayed. All I wanted to do was go home.

Jasper took me to the house and insisted on redressing my cheek. I didn't think it was necessary, but I knew it was something he needed to do. He hadn't been there to protect me, but he could care for me now. After he was done, I told him everything that had happened.

We had a quiet meal and what would've been a relaxing evening if I'd been able to stop wondering what Henley had for me. I knew Jasper was thinking about it too, but we didn't talk about it. We didn't speculate. We sat on the couch together and tried to distract ourselves from what was coming. It wasn't until we were in bed, in the dark, that Jasper asked about it.

"Do you want me to come with you tomorrow?" He had his arms around me, his fingers tracing lazy circles around my nipple. It was a hard point under my thin cotton nightshirt. "I've got almost everything organized at the clinic. I can go in later."

I shook my head. "No, you should finish things up this week so you can open next week. Mr. Henley said it was something good."

"You'll call me as soon as you leave?" His voice was starting to take on that thick sound that happened just before he fell asleep.

"I'll call you," I promised. My own eyelids were heavy.

He made a sound that I interpreted as a thank you and his arms tightened around me as his breathing slowed. I let myself relax back against him and I gradually slipped under.

Mr. Henley didn't usually start seeing clients until nine, but he'd asked me to come in at eight. I wasn't sure how long the meeting would take, but Principal Sanders had assured me he'd have me covered for the whole day. I had plenty of sick days so I didn't have to worry about that. I figured I'd see where things went with Henley and decide then if I wanted to head in to work for the rest of the day. If I didn't feel like it, maybe I'd go see if Jasper wanted to go out to lunch.

There were two other cars in the little parking lot when I pulled in and I recognized the small red one that belonged to Henley. The other one looked like a rental. I parked next to that one and headed inside. Gloria, Mr. Henley's receptionist, gave me a wide smile and waved me in to the lawyer's office. She was on the phone, so I didn't stop to chat like I usually did. I'd been in here enough over the last few months that I'd gotten to know a bit about her family. She had a grandson in the Marines, a pug named Domino and was going to go on a cruise in the spring.

I knocked on Mr. Henley's door, opening it after he called for me to come in. As soon as I stepped inside, I saw that he wasn't alone.

Henley was sitting behind his desk and another man was sitting in one of the two chairs across from him. They both stood when I entered. The other man was tall, easily over six feet, and his lanky frame made him seem even taller. He had that gaunt look of someone who'd lost a great deal of weight in a short period of time. His clothes hung on him despite the fact that they'd obviously been tailor-made for him. They were clearly expensive, but now they were worn, used. His sandy brown hair was short and thinning, his dark eyes intelligent.

"Shae Lockwood, I'd like you to meet Matthew Purcell."

"Mr. Purcell." I stepped forward and held out my hand. I wasn't sure how this man who I'd never seen before was going to help me, but I knew Henley would explain.

"Ms. Lockwood." His voice was gravelly, but tired.

"Please, sit." Mr. Henley gestured towards the

chairs.

I sat next to Mr. Purcell and turned towards my lawyer.

"I'm going to let Mr. Purcell explain why he's here." Henley nodded at the other man.

"Eighteen months ago, I was living in Sacramento with my wife Annabeth and our two daughters," he began.

I tapped my fingers against my leg impatiently, but I didn't interrupt. There had to be a point to this. Henley wouldn't have brought me here otherwise.

"I was the CEO of a large real estate company and was working late, like usual. When I walked outside, there was a woman standing next to my car. I didn't recognize her right away. Why should I have? She'd been a drunken mistake one night nearly a decade ago."

My pulse began to pick up. I thought I knew where this was going, but I didn't allow myself to hope. I had to hear him say it.

"She told me I had a daughter."

"Jenny," I said softly.

He nodded. "She had a picture of the little girl. She told me that I was going to take care of them or she was going to tell my wife about the affair."

I wanted to think poorly of him. He had, after all, cheated on his wife with Aime Vargas...who'd been cheating on Allen at the time. I couldn't do it though. Something about the way he was talking made me think that there was more to his story.

"I'd already told my wife about it," he said with a sad smile. "I'd told her the day after it happened. I'd gone to rehab and we'd moved past it after a year of counseling. When Aime found out that she couldn't blackmail me that way, she said if I didn't pay her, she'd make sure my girls knew what I'd done. She'd ruin my life."

I felt an unexpected pang of sympathy.

"I told her to go to hell."

That was a sentiment I could definitely understand.

"She brought Jenny to see me two days later, and once I'd looked at her, I couldn't tell Aime to go away again."

I knew the feeling. It had been the thought of that little girl that had made me try to calm Aime down yesterday.

"So I gave her some money," Purcell continued. "But it wasn't enough. She came back for more, saying if I didn't give it to her, she'd take me to court for back child support. My company was starting to fail and I didn't have more to give. I still had to take care of my wife and girls. When I told her I couldn't write her another check, she told me that she'd called an attorney. I'd already decided that would be fine. I wasn't going to just take her word for it that Jenny was mine. I needed to know for sure."

I glanced at Mr. Henley, but his face was impassive, not revealing a thing.

"When I told Aime that I wanted a paternity test, she started to get edgy which made me suspect that she wasn't entirely sure I was the father after all."

A part of me wondered how many guys Aime

had scammed, how many men she'd been involved with while she and Allen had been together. A flare of anger went through me. Allen had been a good man. He'd deserved better.

"I'd finally gotten her to agree to a test – if I gave her five thousand dollars – when everything went wrong." He rubbed his hand over his head. "My company tanked. I lost everything. The only assets left belonged to my wife and I wasn't about to ask her for money."

"So Aime left," I guessed.

Purcell nodded. "She ran without a word."

I looked at Henley. "That means Aime has a history of accusing wealthy men of being Jenny's father."

"It's even better than that," he said. He nodded at Purcell. "Go ahead."

I turned back to Purcell.

"I'd had a bad feeling that something was going to happen. Aime hadn't exactly proven herself to be the most reliable person," Purcell continued, a sheepish expression on his face. "Before she'd run, I'd managed to get a few minutes alone with Jenny and convinced her to let me swab her mouth with one of those kits."

My hands curled into fists, my nails biting into my palms.

"I got the results two weeks after they vanished," Purcell said. "I'm Jenny's father."

All of the air rushed out of my lungs and I slumped back in my chair.

I'd already known that Allen wasn't Jenny's

180

father, but to have someone sitting here and stating that he, in fact, was...

I looked at Henley.

"I've drawn up the paperwork, including a statement from Mr. Purcell to go along with the medical information. I managed to get us an emergency hearing in forty-five minutes."

"An emergency hearing?" My head was spinning. I was still trying to wrap my head around the fact that Aime had tried to scam someone else and he'd actually turned out to be Jenny's father.

"I may have lost my business," Purcell said. "But I still have friends, and a couple of them happen to be in law enforcement. I asked them to let me know if anything came up with the name Aime Vargas."

"Her lawsuit," I said as it clicked. "When her name went into the system, someone contacted you."

Purcell nodded. "I've been looking for her ever since I got the test results back, and I'm always too late. She's tried this in two other states, but both times, she got spooked and ran."

I glanced at Henley. "She could go to jail for this, right? Extortion or something like that?"

Henley nodded. "Mr. Purcell here has the names of the other men she tried to scam."

"But more than that, I want to get custody of Jenny," Purcell put in.

My respect for him rose. He may have screwed up and cheated on his wife, but it looked like he was doing all he could to make up for it. And now he wanted to protect the daughter he hadn't known about.

"Hence the emergency hearing," Henley interjected. "This is the closest Mr. Purcell has been and we don't want Aime getting wind of it. I had a judge that owed me a favor so I was able to file a joint petition, one for Mr. Purcell to take emergency custody of Jenny and another one to have Aime's suit against you dropped."

"It could be done today?" I asked, hardly daring to believe it.

Henley gave me a warm smile. "There's a very good chance that we could leave that hearing with Aime's suit against you dismissed, Jenny ordered into Mr. Purcell's custody, and charges filed against Aime."

I stared at him. He was serious. This really could be all over in a matter of hours.

Still, I'd believe it when I saw it.

# Chapter 22

I was in a daze when I walked out of the courtroom. The judge had heard Henley's presentation regarding recent paternity evidence. He hadn't even bothered to ask where Allen's DNA had come from. Instead, he'd read the statements, asked Mr. Purcell if he'd be willing to testify under oath about his relationship with Aime Vargas and his relationship to Jenny. When Purcell had said that he was, the judge had studied him for a moment, then ruled that Aime's suit against Allen's estate was dismissed.

After that, the judge listened to Purcell's petition for custody. I was still in a bit of shock when the judge ruled that Jenny Vargas was to be taken into the state's custody while an inquiry was conducted into the whole situation. While I wasn't planning on staying up-to-date on the custody issue, I was still glad to hear that there was a good chance Purcell could get custody, especially if the charges against Aime stuck.

As I walked away from the courthouse, I pulled my phone out of my purse. It was about the time

Jasper usually went to lunch. I made the call while I walked to my car. I gave Jasper the basics over the phone and promised him details when I saw him. I was still trying to process it all.

I didn't go to work. There were only a couple hours left in the day and I doubted I'd be any good to my students. So I went home. I stopped at the vineyard office to check in with Jacques and see how the preparation for harvest was coming. By the time I was halfway back to the house, I'd all but forgotten what we'd talked about. I couldn't seem to focus on anything.

Then I saw Jasper's car and smiled. I walked into the house and he was there, a bottle of beer in each hand. Without a word, he handed one to me. I took a long drink and let him lead me over to the couch. While I told him all of the details of what had happened at Henley's office, he didn't say anything. He took off my shoes and began to massage my feet.

I made a pleased sound as his thumb pressed against the sole of my foot, the pressure point releasing some of the tension in my body. He smiled down at me as he continued to rub. His hands moved up to my ankles, then my calves.

"Busy day," he said, finally breaking the silence.

I agreed, "It was."

"I'd like to do something for you," he said, his voice soft. "Will you let me?"

I didn't have to think about it. I nodded. I let out a surprised squeak as he swept me into his arms. His eyes met mine as he carried me up the stairs.

"Do you trust me?"

I trusted him. Completely.

Which was how I'd ended up on my bed, naked...and blindfolded.

I was face down on the bed and I could feel Jasper kneeling over me. He'd slowly been working his way up my body, his strong fingers kneading deep into my muscles. By the time he reached my ass, my limbs were starting to feel like rubber. He found every knot and worked them until they were gone. As he worked his way up my spine, I let out a shuddering breath. How had I not known he could do this?

"Feeling better?" His lips were next to my ear, his low voice sending a rush of arousal through me.

"Much," I breathed.

"I'm just getting started."

I could almost hear the smile.

"When I'm done with the massage, I'm going to go down on you until you beg me to fuck you."

A shiver went through me.

"And then I'm going to take you long and slow. Make love to you until we both can't stand it anymore."

"Fuck." The word was strangled.

His thumbs pressed hard on my spine, then moved across my shoulder blades. "And that blindfold is going to stay on so you can't see a single thing. Only feel it."

This was, I suddenly realized, as much a test of trust for Jasper as it was for me. Blindfolded, I had to trust that he'd only do things I wanted him to do, but because I couldn't see him, he had to trust I wasn't imagining that he was Allen.

His hands moved down my arms, massaging all the way to my fingertips before moving to my neck and across my shoulders. After a few minutes, he gently turned me onto my back and started at my feet again. This time, however, I could feel the teasing edge to his touch as he made his way up my thighs. His thumbs brushed close to my pussy and I shivered. He chuckled as his fingers moved to my hips, then up my sides. When he cupped my breasts, I arched into his hands.

"You have the most amazing body," he said as he traced circles around my breasts and up to my nipples. By the time he took the tips between his fingers and thumbs, they were hard, aching for attention.

I gasped as wet heat enveloped one nipple. My eyes closed behind the blindfold, letting all of my senses concentrate on the point where he was applying hard, steady suction. It was like he had a straight line from my breast to the core of me, every pull of his mouth sending a new jolt of pleasure through me.

Then it was gone and the cool air against my wet skin made goosebumps break out across my flesh. Lips and teeth began to work on the other nipple, scraping and licking. Every time I tried to lift my hands to touch him, he pressed them back to the bed, holding them there until I stopped resisting.

"Jas," I breathed out his name as he shifted, placing open-mouthed kisses down my stomach.

His tongue circled my belly button, making me squirm until his hands grasped my hips, stilling my movements.

"I could spend the rest of my life touching you, tasting you, being inside you, and it still wouldn't be enough." His voice was low, almost reverent.

I caught my breath as he pressed his mouth against me in an almost-chaste kiss. Then I felt the tip of his tongue ghosting over my slit, not pushing inside, just barely touching the sensitive skin. I tried to move my hips, to force more friction, but he held me tight, forcing me to remain still as he leisurely licked every inch before finally parting my folds and letting his tongue dip inside.

I wanted to touch him, to put my hands on his head so I could feel his hair between my fingers, so I could pull him against me until he gave me what I wanted, but he'd made it clear that I wasn't allowed to move. I had to do something though, had to grab something more solid than my sheets. I stretched my arms above my head and gripped the intricate spirals that decorated my headboard. My fingers tightened almost painfully as Jasper moved again, this time spreading my legs wider and settling them around his shoulders so that my heels rested on his spine, right between his shoulder blades.

As his tongue began to work its magic on my clit, the sounds that came out of my mouth were ones that would've made me blush if I'd thought about it.

But I wasn't thinking about the noises I was making or how exposed I was. The only thing close to a coherent thought I could manage was somewhere in the realm of "please don't stop."

I didn't have to say it though because it was clear he wasn't about to stop. When my first climax hit me, I cried out, but he didn't even pause from what he was doing. His tongue worked around my entrance, darting inside before moving back up to my clit. The muscles in my arms strained as I tried to twist away, needing more, needing less, needing something I couldn't articulate. One orgasm rolled into another until I couldn't tell if it was the same one or multiple ones, only that I was sure I would explode if it didn't stop.

Yet, while it was almost too much, it wasn't quite enough. I needed more than just the pleasure his mouth and fingers were giving me. I needed him inside me.

"Please, Jas," I begged. "Please."

"Please what?" His fingers continued to stroke me as he spoke.

"I need..." I slammed my hand against the headboard as he curled his fingers inside me. "Please, Jas."

"What do you need, Shae?" He kissed the inside of my thigh. "Tell me what you need."

"Fuck me." The words burst out of me as I came again. "Fuck me, Jas. Please."

I gasped as he pulled his fingers out of me, but the gasp became a breathless wail when he filled me with one thrust. He groaned and I felt the weight of his body as he leaned over me.

"So fucking tight."

He wrapped his arms around me as he waited for me to adjust to him. His breath was hot against my neck, his hair brushing against my cheek. I could smell the mingled scents of sex and the spicy aftershave he wore. I let go of the headboard and put my hands on his shoulders. When he didn't move them away, I slid my hands over his back, loving the feel of his skin, of the muscles rippling underneath.

"You feel so good," he murmured as he kissed the side of my throat.

I made a noise that I hoped he interpreted as agreement because I wasn't sure I could manage an actual word, let alone a sentence. My skin felt like it was on fire as it slid against his, my nipples hard as they rubbed against his chest. Every inch of me was practically vibrating from everything I was feeling.

And then he began to move.

His strokes were as slow and deep as he'd promised, each one pushing me closer and closer to the edge, higher than I'd been before. I wrapped my legs around his waist, my heels resting just under his ass so I could feel those firm muscles flexing as he thrust into me. My nails bit into his back when I came the first time and I heard him swear, his hips jerking against me as his rhythm faltered.

He held himself still as I spasmed around him, not starting to move again until the pleasure started to fade. He built it back up again and again, each time waiting out my orgasm without allowing himself release. I could feel the strain as he fought back his own needs until, finally, he couldn't hold back anymore. When I came again, he kept moving, driving into me faster and harder until he buried himself deep inside me.

"Shae," he cried out my name, his face pressed against my shoulder.

I wrapped my arms around him, holding him to me as our bodies shuddered against each other. As I started to come down, what little strength I'd had left began to fade, leaving my muscles weak and limp. Still, I clung to him, wanting to keep him close.

The darkness closed in fast and I felt him moving even as I started to fall asleep. I wasn't worried though. It was Jasper. He would take care of me.

I was falling hard and fast, and I knew that should have scared the hell out of me. But it didn't. It was Jasper. I knew he'd never do anything to hurt me, never betray me. He was a constant, reassuring presence that I never wanted to lose. I trusted him.

# Chapter 23

I finally had to admit that if I waited for Jasper to finish his own unpacking, it'd be Christmas before he got everything sorted. Though, if I was being honest, it wasn't entirely his fault. Since he'd moved in, he'd worked full days either at his father's practice or at the clinic, come home for dinner and then done some small repairs or yard work while I did school stuff. Generally, by the time the sun went down, we were both too exhausted to do more than sit on the couch and stare at the tv.

Principal Sanders had been surprised when I hadn't called off on Friday too, but I'd needed the distraction. I was grateful for how things had gone with Aime and Jenny, relieved that it was one less legal issue I had to worry about. I did, however, still have the Lockwoods to deal with.

The judge had set a date for the ruling about Allen's trust. January tenth. Mr. Henley told me that it was actually sooner than he'd expected, but I wasn't looking forward to waiting another two months for this to be over. The Lockwoods had called too, leaving half a dozen messages that all, in one way or another, told me to just sign over the trust and the vineyard or they'd drag this out until nothing was left of Allen's estate.

All that had happened since I'd gotten home from school and I still had at least another half hour before Jasper got home, and that was if he left the clinic on time. I wasn't upset though. If he was still going to open on Monday, I knew he needed to finish things up today or he'd need to go in over the weekend.

Dinner was already cooking in the oven, but I needed something to take my mind off of things until then. Since there were still several boxes of Jasper's things stacked in the home office, I decided that would be the best use of my time.

The first box looked like tax information, receipts and things like that. I set it aside. We'd need to get him some better place to file his receipts. Maybe I could convince him to switch to the accounting software Allen and my accountant used.

The second box held odds and ends and I pulled it down to the floor so I could sit next to it. I smiled as I pulled out a Little League trophy. Neither Allen nor I had known Jasper as a child, though I was sure Allen had heard stories over the years. I hadn't, not really. There was so much about him I didn't know.

The metal plating on the bottom of the trophy had his name, and underneath it was "3rd Place Willow Creek Summer Camp." It didn't have a year and I wondered how old Jasper had been when he'd gone to camp. I was a bit surprised that he'd kept a baseball trophy since I'd never seen him display any sort of interest in sports. I knew he'd go running sometimes before he left for work or after dinner, but that was it.

My heart clenched as I pulled a picture frame out next. It was Allen and Jasper, their arms slung around each other's necks, smiles on their faces. I didn't know where the picture had been taken or even if it had been after Allen and I had met. They looked happy.

I brushed my thumb across the glass covering Allen's face and felt my lips curve into a smile. It was a wistful one, but not entirely sad. I was glad I could remember him like that. Happy, smiling.

I set the picture aside. Jasper had already put some of his things around the house, but there hadn't been any pictures. I made a mental note to ask him if he wanted to put this one somewhere we could both see it. After my – for the lack of a better word – temper tantrum when I'd trashed all of my pictures, I'd bought a few new frames and put some of the photos back up, including one of Jasper with Allen and me at our wedding.

The rest of the box was full of much of the same. Little bits of Jasper's past, giving me a glimpse of the little boy Jasper had been. A partially burnt candle from what I assumed was a tenth birthday cake. A broken toy plane. A handful of seashells and rocks. A tarnished and dented key chain. Another picture, this time of a much-younger Jasper with a dark-haired teenager I didn't recognize. Most likely the friend Jasper had lost when he was a senior in high school. He never talked about what had happened or the boy who'd died.

I put most of the things back into the box, leaving out only the picture of Allen and Jasper. I put it on the desk and opened the bottom box. Stacks of files had been haphazardly stuffed into the box as if Jasper had just tossed them in. Knowing him, he'd done just that. Where Allen had been meticulous to the point of obsessive, Jasper was only that careful when it came to dealing with people. He was much less particular about filing, which was why he'd been more than happy to hire Georgia at the clinic.

I wasn't going to read any of the information, but I couldn't let the files stay in there like that either. I didn't know how he planned to file things from his father's practice, but I could at least put things together so that it would be easier for him once he decided what to do.

The box was wide enough to fit the files on end, with the patients' names facing up. I tried not to look at them as I arranged them, not bothering to try alphabetizing or anything like that. I was almost done when his name caught my eye.

Not Jasper's name.

Allen's.

He was my husband, I reasoned. And he was gone. There was no logical reason to keep things hidden anymore. I took the file and stood, walking over to the desk. I didn't look away from Allen's name as I sat down. My stomach was churning. I knew it wasn't the right thing to do. These were confidential. It would be violating Jasper's trust as well as Allen's. But Allen was gone. And I had a right to know. Allen's letter had said he was sick and that Jasper had known, but I had the files right in front of me. Files that would give me more than just a few words to try to explain why he'd left me in such a cruel and sudden way.

Jasper never needed to know.

I set the file down on the desk and opened it.

The top file had Allen's basic information. Latest insurance. Contact information. Medical history.

I skimmed all of that. I already knew it. The date on the top was from a couple weeks before he'd died. Underneath was what I really wanted and I read through each bit carefully.

Then I read them all again because I couldn't believe what I was seeing.

X-rays with post-it notes confirming everything was clear.

A CT scan reading that said no issues had been found.

Blood work results that listed two pages worth of tests run.

His blood pressure had been a bit high, but not dangerously so. Everything else had been within a healthy range.

Brain scans and even a spinal tap.

All clear.

I was no doctor, but I couldn't see anything in here that said Allen had been sick. It didn't make any sense. Allen had written that he'd gone to Jasper for tests because he'd known Jasper would sign off on his health even if something was wrong.

I frowned as I looked further into the file. There were half a dozen physicals Allen had done over the past decade, all without any indication of problems.

There had to be something missing. This couldn't be it.

I shut the file and leaned back in the chair.

"Dammit," I muttered.

I just wanted answers. I was trying to move on, but it was hard to do when I still couldn't quite wrap my head around Allen having committed suicide because he was sick. I needed to see it for myself.

I'd researched the disease Allen had mentioned in his letter and I'd actually had a couple nightmares about it. It was horrible, taking someone from seemingly perfect health to death in months, weeks. And it did it in a brutal way. Loss of motor function. Recognition. Speech. I'd seen families write that it was like watching the person they loved wasting away right in front of them.

I wouldn't have wanted that for Allen, and I definitely wouldn't have wanted to have to watch him go through it. But I still needed to see it in black and white, needed to see that diagnosis.

Then I saw it.

Allen's laptop.

In all of my cleaning, I hadn't done anything with it. It wasn't like clothes or things I'd wanted to donate or like his favorite foods that I'd thrown away. This was an expensive piece of equipment. I'd just left it. I had my own laptop so I hadn't planned on using it, but I'd completely forgotten to figure out what to do with it.

I plugged it in and turned it on. I didn't know what I was expecting to find, but I knew there had to be something that could answer my questions.

I skimmed through a few files and then booted up the email program. New junk mail and newsletters flooded in and I spent the next fifteen minutes wading through all of that before I reached Allen's last correspondence.

The first two I opened were from customers of the winery who'd kept in touch with Allen, wanting to know about the latest batch. Then there was one from his brother Marcus regarding their father's health and how Allen's absence wasn't helping things.

My heart nearly stopped when the next email came up on my screen.

*I agree with you that you should take out a bigger insurance policy. You want to make sure that Shae is taken care of, especially if you think your parents would try to take the vineyard if something happened to you. Come see me and I'll do some tests. If there is something wrong with you, I'll help you out with the insurance. Shae deserves to be taken care of. And don't worry about trying to help me out with the clinic. I'll be fine. We need to make sure you're okay first. I'll get the money somehow.*

*Jasper.*

Jasper.

He'd known about the insurance. He'd encouraged Allen to take it out. And he'd known that Allen had wanted to help him with the clinic.

I looked at the file and my stomach churned.

Were the files in the folder the ones Jasper had sent to the insurance company and he'd trashed the real ones just in case someone wanted to look at Allen's records?

I supposed that was possible, but I couldn't see Jasper not keeping the real records somewhere else. He was too good of a doctor for that.

Another thought was forming in my mind and it was one I really didn't want to consider.

The thought that these files were Allen's true test results and Jasper had lied to Allen about the diagnosis, knowing how his best friend would react. For all I knew, he'd not only encouraged Allen to get the insurance, but had encouraged him to end things on his own terms.

I'd gone through the file and email to get answers, but now all I had was more questions.

# Chapter 24

I spent the next hour arguing with myself about what I was going to do with the information I'd found. Part of me felt guilty about what I'd done to get it, but most of me was pissed off. Pissed and getting even angrier with every passing minute. Angry at myself for thinking the worst of Jasper. Angry at Jasper for having this file.

Hell, I was angry at the file for existing.

How fucked up was that? I was angry at the test results and papers in that file because they made me even more confused than I'd already been. Confused and doubting. I hated that I was doubting again, doubting what I knew, doubting myself.

Doubting Jasper.

I didn't want to doubt him. He was too important to me. I had friends, acquaintances and family, though the numbers were definitely small, but I didn't have anyone else like him. I cared about him. Trusted him.

I sighed. Who was I trying to kid? I was falling for him, and I had been for a while.

And now this.

By the time Jasper came in, I'd almost made up my mind to let the whole thing go. To accept that Allen was gone and it didn't matter what those records said. I had a letter from him, telling me what he'd believed. That could be the truth.

Then Jasper looked at the file sitting on the coffee table and I knew letting it go wasn't an option now.

"Where did that come from?" His voice was flat.

I crossed my arms and shifted my weight from one foot to the other. "I thought I'd unpack some of the boxes in the office." I paused, but he didn't say anything so I continued, "The last box had some files thrown in it."

"So you just thought you'd go through my patient files?"

I could hear the undercurrent of anger in his question.

"No." I shook my head. I was upset, but I needed him to know what happened before I addressed what was in that file. "I only straightened them. That's all. I didn't even alphabetize them because I didn't want to look at the names."

He gave me a hard look, then nodded. "All right. Then what's that?" He gestured towards the file again.

"It's Allen's."

A cold silence fell between us and I rubbed my hands over my arms. Jasper took a slow breath and then let it out, but his eyes were still blank, unreadable.

"He was my husband," I said, feeling the

pressure in my chest start to build again. "I had a right to know."

Jasper frowned. "I told you everything, Shae."

He walked over to stand in front of me, but he didn't touch me. The tension between us was palpable.

"Did you?" My voice was sharper than I'd intended it to be. "Did you tell me everything, Jasper?"

His mouth flattened. "Yes, Shae. When you got that letter, I told you everything. I've never lied to you."

I picked up the file and slapped it against his chest. "Then why don't you explain to me why there's nothing in this file about Jasper being sick. Is this the file you sent to the insurance company? Tell me that it is."

He opened the file and glanced at the papers inside. After just a few moments, he shook his head. "I don't know what to tell you."

"How about the truth?" I asked. He wasn't denying anything, only flipping through the file with a confused look on his face. "I found your email."

"What email?" He dropped the file onto the coffee table. "Shae, I don't know what's going on here, but you need to believe me. I've never seen that file before. I sent an old report to the insurance company, yes, but I didn't keep anything because I could lose my license if anyone found out what I'd done."

He was right about that, but the file was right there. It was hard to argue with something that was

201

right in front of me.

"You didn't email Allen and tell him to take out that extra insurance policy?" I put my hands on my hips. "You didn't tell him that you'd find the money for your clinic somewhere else? That taking care of him was the most important thing and that you'd help him get insurance if he really was sick?"

"No." Jasper shook his head. "I never said any of that. I swear, Shae, I only suspected about the policy. I didn't know about him wanting to give me money for the clinic until you told me."

"I read the email, Jasper." I swallowed hard.

"What are you talking about?" His eyes were darkening, and not from any sort of lust or desire.

"The email on Allen's computer," I said. I glared at Jasper, wondering how he could've done this. How he could've lied to me. "I still have his laptop. I read it."

"I didn't send a damn email!" Jasper's voice was harsh. "Why would I lie to you? I told you what I did and you forgave me for it. Why the hell would I lie about something like this?"

"I don't know!" My eyes burned. "But the file's there. The email's there."

"Shae..." He ran his hand through his hair. "Why would I do anything to risk what we have? I love you."

I shook my head. "You say that but—"

"I've been in love with you almost from the moment Allen introduced us."

I stopped and stared. That couldn't be true. Maybe he'd said that he loved me sort of fast, but nothing about our relationship was normal. We'd found each other under strange and intense circumstances. That was all. He'd been my friend and things had just gone from there.

He hadn't thought about me as anything other than a friend before...

He'd kissed me.

The memory shocked me.

I remembered, of course, the first time Jasper and I had slept together, how accepting he'd been of whatever I wanted to do with what had happened. I'd been the one to kiss him then and it had been impulsive. I'd been drunk and lonely, but I'd wanted him.

But that hadn't been the first time we'd kissed. He'd kissed me before that. Two months before. Was it possible that the reason he'd done it, the reason he'd freaked out so badly afterwards, was because he'd been wanting to do it before Allen had died?

"You what?" The words were barely a whisper.

"I've been in love with you for eight years, Shae." Jasper's voice was as soft as mine, but he wasn't looking at me. "But you were Allen's."

"Why...you..." This was not how I'd expected this conversation to go. Or any conversation to go for that matter.

"Like I said. You were Allen's." He shrugged. "And after...it just didn't seem important."

"Not important." I kept staring at him as my brain tried to process what he was saying.

How could I not have known?

Had Allen known?

I couldn't believe that Allen would've known and not said something, but how does a person tell his girlfriend – his wife – that his best friend is in love with her? If Allen had known, how could he and Jasper still have stayed friends?

But that wasn't the point. None of this was the point, was it?

It didn't matter what Allen had known or hadn't known. It didn't matter that Jasper'd had this...crush on me for years. Or even if he really had loved me. It didn't change anything. I had to focus on the matter at hand.

Unless...

An icy hand squeezed my heart and I suddenly found it hard to breathe.

Jasper had been in love with me for years.

I had chosen Allen.

The fact that I hadn't known it had been a choice didn't really matter. I'd picked Allen, which meant I hadn't picked Jasper.

For eight years, he'd wanted someone he couldn't have. He'd watched me fall in love with his best friend. Watched us get engaged. Get married.

He'd watched the woman he said he loved get married to his best friend.

I couldn't imagine how hard that had been.

And that was where the question came in.

Had it been too much?

Had all the years of watching and wanting been too much for him?

I'd always thought of him as this controlled, quiet man, but since we'd been together, I'd seen the passion in him, seen the intensity. Was it possible that it had been there all along? Bubbling under the surface and he'd simply snapped?

Had Allen come to him and said he'd thought he was sick...and Jasper had seen it as an opportunity?

The idea made me sick to my stomach, but I couldn't stop it from taking root.

Had Jasper done the tests, seen that Allen was fine, but then thought that maybe this was his chance? Had he known his friend well enough to know that if Allen thought he was going to die a horrible, slow death, he'd end it? And if Jasper had known that, had he decided that the best way to get what he wanted was to tell Allen that he was dying?

It was too horrible to consider, but there it was.

Had Jasper wanted me enough to set in motion my husband's suicide?

Had he maybe even suggested the option to Allen?

I swallowed hard and rubbed at my arms again, but the friction did nothing against the chill inside me.

"Jasper, tell me the truth. All of it."

"I have." He shook his head. "How can you not believe me? After everything..."

I looked down at the file and then back up at Jasper. He'd lied to me before. Now I was finding out that everything in our past was essentially a lie too. He'd pretended to be my friend when he'd always wanted more. How could I believe he was telling the truth now?

"Get out."

He stared at me even though I knew he'd heard me.

"I mean it, Jasper." I made my voice as hard as I could. "I don't believe you. I don't trust you."

He flinched.

"Leave."

He held my gaze for a moment and then turned around and walked away without a word. It wasn't until the door closed behind him that I let myself give in to the tears.

# Chapter 25

I didn't sleep at all that night.

I'd already spent so much of the past five months crying that I hated it. I hated the physical feeling of it as much or more than the emotional part of it. But I couldn't stop myself. I was torn up inside. I wanted to believe Jasper, but there were so many things stacked against him. And there was no way to find out the truth. Allen couldn't vouch for his friend, couldn't tell me if Jasper was lying or being honest. It was only Jasper's word against the physical evidence I had.

I spent the rest of Friday night and into the early hours of Saturday morning curled up in my bed, staring into the darkness and wondering how I'd gotten here. How, in less than a year, had things gone so wrong? I was supposed to be with my husband, trying to get pregnant or planning for a baby. I wasn't supposed to be alone in my house, crying over the betrayal of my new lover, my husband's best friend.

My life was so fucked up.

When I thought about it, I had to admit that was

a large part of why I was so upset. Things had just started to look like they were getting back to normal. Sure, there had still been a few things that still needed to be worked out, but it wasn't the chaos and uncertainty of before. I had my home. No one was going to take that from me. I was teaching and the routine was familiar and good. Things with Jasper had been solid and we'd been falling into the rhythm of living together.

Now it had all gone to shit.

Again.

I knew I had to accept responsibility for parts of it. I had been the one to go through Jasper's files and then read Allen's emails. But, whether or not I'd done either of those things, the past had still happened. Allen had still believed he was dying and he'd still killed himself. Whatever Jasper's role in that had been, it wouldn't have changed if I'd left the box alone and never found out any of it.

My relationship with Jasper was my own fault though. The first night we'd slept together, I'd kissed him. I'd forgiven him after I'd gotten Allen's letter in the mail. I'd been the one who'd kept asking him to come around since the beginning, simply because I hadn't wanted to be alone. I'd been the one to push things forward. I'd asked him to move in with me. My heartbreak had been my own doing.

Now I had another choice to make and whatever happened as a result would rest solely on me.

It was that decision that actually kept me awake all night, not crying over Jasper and Allen. I had to decide what to do with the new information I'd stumbled upon. I hadn't taken Allen's letter to the police because I hadn't wanted Jasper to get in trouble for falsifying Allen's medical records. But now it looked like Jasper hadn't done that. It had been Allen he'd lied to, not the insurance company.

All of the choices and possibilities ran circles in my mind as the minutes slowly ticked past. When it finally hit five o'clock, I knew there was no point in staying in bed any longer, no matter how much I wanted to pull the blankets over my head and forget everything that had happened.

Forgetting, unfortunately, wasn't really an option. Even if I stayed in bed, I'd be constantly reminded that the bed was empty. That the two men I'd brought into it were gone.

I took a long, hot shower and the white noise of the water helped calm my thoughts for a short while. As soon as I climbed out of the shower, however, everything came rushing back. I knew the longer I waited to make my decision, the harder it would be. And if I did go to the police, I was sure that the detectives working Allen's case would find my delay curious. I knew at least Detective Reed was suspicious of me. I'd gotten the impression that he was the kind of man who had a chip on his shoulder when it came to women in general. I hoped Detective Rheingard was more interested in justice than blaming me, but if I kept putting things off, even he would have to wonder why.

It wasn't until I started thinking about how the two detectives would react to me bringing in the letter and files that I realized I was seriously considering turning over evidence that could lead to Jasper being arrested for Allen's death.

I sank down on the edge of my bed, my hand automatically continuing to towel dry my hair. Could I do that? I wasn't one hundred percent sure that Jasper had done anything, but the suspicions were there. Was that enough to possibly ruin his life? But if he had done it, didn't I want to see him arrested, to see him pay for taking Allen from me? How much was justice for my husband worth?

That was the real question, I knew.

I'd told Jasper I didn't trust him, to leave, and that might have ruined things between us for good, but there was always the possibility that I was wrong. That he hadn't done anything and, in the far reaches of possibility, would still want to be with me.

If I went to the police, however, that slim chance would disappear, of that I had no doubt. It was one thing to react in anger and grief, another to make a deliberate decision that could ruin his life.

But if there was a chance that I was right and Jasper had set things in motion for Allen to kill himself, then I owed it to Allen to go to the police.

Didn't I?

I buried my head in my hands.

When Jasper and I had first gotten together, I'd felt a bit guilty, but I'd known any feelings of having betrayed Allen had been residual. Allen was gone. Jasper was here. I hadn't been choosing one over the other. I'd gone with how I'd felt. This, however, was making me choose. Justice for Allen or freedom for Jasper. That was simplifying it quite a bit since I had no way of knowing for certain what the outcome would be, but no matter what choice I made, I'd be putting one man above the other.

I cared about Jasper. I truly did. But the physical evidence was there. And I'd been with Allen for eight years. If Jasper was guilty and got away with it, I'd never forgive myself. But if he was innocent, surely the detectives would find that out. I'd lose him, but at least he wouldn't be in trouble for something he hadn't done.

I had to trust in the system, right?

Besides, how could the police run a thorough investigation if they didn't have all the evidence?

I knew I was trying to justify it to myself, but the logical arguments were hard to push away.

I dressed and went into the office, pulling up Jasper's email on Allen's laptop. I printed two copies, putting one in the desk and taking the other one with me as I got Allen's letter and made a copy of that. The copy went into the desk and the original joined the copy of the email. Once I had that, I went out into the living room and picked up the file.

My heart was racing as I walked into the police station twenty minutes later. The desk sergeant gestured towards the back, but I already knew where Reed and Rheingard's desks were. I didn't actually want to talk to either one, but I knew I had to give these files to someone and if I went straight to them, maybe they'd finally realize that I'd had nothing to do with Allen's death.

"Mrs. Lockwood," Detective Rheingard said as he stood.

Detective Reed was already on his feet, leaning against his desk, but he straightened as I got closer. He glanced over at the other detective, their expressions unreadable.

"I have some information that might be important." I wasn't about to tell them what I suspected. If Jasper was guilty, the detectives would find it on their own. If he wasn't, they'd know that Allen had committed suicide. Either way, the case would be closed.

I held out the files and Detective Rheingard took them.

"We were actually just going to come see you," Reed said.

My stomach twisted. That didn't sound good.

Rheingard set the papers and file down on his desk and glanced at his partner. Reed nodded.

"Shae Lockwood," Rheingard began. "You're under arrest for the death of Allen Lockwood. You have the right to remain silent..."

**The End**

**Don't miss the thrilling conclusion to the story in A Wicked Truth, release September 15$^{th}$.**

# All series from M. S. Parker

Casual Encounter Box Set
Sinful Desires Box Set
Twisted Affair Box Set
Club Prive Vol. 1 to 5
French Connection (Club Prive) Vol. 1 to 3
Chasing Perfection Vol. 1 to 4
Pleasures Series
Exotic Desires Series
Serving HIM Series
Pure Lust Series
A Wicked Lie
A Wicked Kiss (Release August 25th)
A Wicked Truth (Release September 15th)

# Acknowledgement

First, I would like to thank all of my readers. Without you, my books would not exist. I truly appreciate each and every one of you.

A big "thanks" goes out to all the Facebook fans, street team, beta readers, and advanced reviewers. You are a HUGE part of the success of the series.

I have to thank my PA, Shannon Hunt. Without you my life would be a complete and utter mess. Also a big thank you goes out to my editor Lynette and my wonderful cover designer, Sinisa. You make my ideas and writing look so good.

# About The Author

*MS Parker*

M. S. Parker is a USA Today Bestselling author and the author of the Erotic Romance series, Club Privè and Chasing Perfection.

Living in Southern California, she enjoys sitting by the pool with her laptop writing on her next spicy romance.

Growing up all she wanted to be was a dancer, actor or author. So far only the latter has come true but M. S. Parker hasn't retired her dancing shoes just yet. She is still waiting for the call for her to appear on Dancing With The Stars.

When M. S. isn't writing, she can usually be found reading– oops, scratch that! She is always writing.

GRAYSLAKE AREA PUBLIC LIBRARY
100 Library Lane
Grayslake, IL 60030

45325786R00123

Made in the USA
Lexington, KY ·
24 September 2015